CLARA BENNETT

SECRET OF THE KUKULKAN TEMPLE

SECOND EDITION
BOOK ONE

RENEE YUKSEL

Illustrated by
KAREN MCKINNEY

To new beginnings in Jesus Christ.

This book is a work of fiction. Although it is based on real events, the author has created characters, names, and places through their imagination or used them fictitiously.

Cover Design: by Karen McKinney

Published by Strolling Donkeys, LLC, 30 N Gould St STE N, Sheridan, WY 82801

WWW.strollingdonkeys.com

Second Edition Published in 2025

Second Edition ISBN-979-8-9989104-2-5

First Edition Published under Renee Habibi in 2015

First Edition ISBN-10 0692600019

First Edition ISBN-13 978-0692600016

❀ Formatted with Vellum

CHAPTER 1

The drive to Calakmul unfolded as a beloved ritual, the tropical forest stretching beyond the car window in an unbroken expanse of green, vibrant under the early January sun. I lowered the window, letting the warm breeze sweep in, rich with the scent of moist soil, fresh leaves, and the faint sweetness of wild orchids. The distant calls of parrots, punctuated by the low hoots of howler monkeys, blended into a natural melody, each sound a note in the jungle's living symphony. I glanced at Daniel, his hazel eyes tracing the horizon, a contented smile softening his features as he absorbed the landscape, our mutual excitement for the journey ahead simmering quietly between us.

Our route spanned nearly 160 miles, culminating at the Puerta Calakmul Hotel, situated at the entrance of the Calakmul Biosphere Reserve, which is home to the ancient Mayan city-state of Calakmul, a powerhouse from 250 to 900 AD. Spanning over 2,500 square miles, the reserve lay 22 miles north of Guatemala, a vast sanctuary of wildlife and historical treasures. My PhD research had drawn us to Calakmul before, each visit deepening my fascination with its stone-carved history, but today's destination was a newly uncovered Mayan ruin, 31 miles northeast, its remote location within the reserve's dense forest keeping it hidden until recent discovery.

Daniel had planned for us to fly solo from Belize to Mexico, a rare chance for solitude before joining our research team at the hotel tonight. The new site, inaccessible by road due to the reserve's protected status, required helicopter transport, as clearing a path was forbidden. The National Institute of Anthropology and History (NIAH) would survey the site to assess its condition before deciding next steps. This process thrilled me with its potential to reveal untouched secrets. Our invitation from NIAH, prompted by our former professor Dr. McAdoo, marked a shift from our Belize government archaeology roles, though his name was notably absent from the official letter.

The prospect of exploring the site sent a surge of anticipation through me, my pulse quickening at the thought of deciphering its ancient structures. In Mexico, the government oversaw all archaeological endeavors, whether conducted by public or private teams, and Dr. McAdoo's leadership promised a meticulous approach. An Englishman with a Cambridge degree, he had taught at Galen University in Belize for 15 years before joining NIAH, his expertise a reassuring foundation as we embarked on this venture. I pictured the site's glyphs, their stories waiting for Maria's translations, a task that would bind our team's efforts.

Arturo, our driver, greeted us at the hotel where we'd stayed after arriving at Manuel Crescencio Rejón International Airport. His white Nissan Versa, its dashboard cluttered with colorful trinkets, was a familiar sight from past Calakmul trips. His animated voice filled the car as he shared theories about the Mayans' decline—overpopulation, warfare, environmental shifts—his enthusiasm infectious. Daniel and I sat in the backseat, our shoulders brushing, the forest blurring past in a mosaic of greens, Arturo's words weaving a historical tapestry that heightened our anticipation for Huntuunich.

I wore jeans and a white peasant top adorned with red floral embroidery, the fabric soft against my cinnamon skin. A silver necklace with a large azalea pendant gleamed at my throat, complemented by a bracelet consisting of turquoise Mayan glyphs, their intricate designs purely decorative. My brown leather gladiator sandals were both practical and stylish, suited for the day's travel. Daniel's quiet compliment, "Red suits you," warmed me, his voice a gentle anchor amidst the journey's excitement, his gaze lingering on my features.

Standing at 5'4", my athletic frame reflected years of hiking and field-work, my ginger hair falling in loose waves to mid-back, framing an oval face with full lips and a small, upturned nose. Daniel often said my almond-shaped amber eyes were my most striking feature, a sentiment that deepened our bond. At 28, my Mestizo and British heritage, with a trace of Greek from my mother, connected me to the region's history, the forest's energy resonating with my own curiosity and resilience.

Daniel, also 28 and of Mestizo-British descent, had a cocoa skin tone, chestnut hair, and hazel eyes, his oval face marked by full lips and a straight, pointed nose. Lean and muscular at 5'9", he wore tan khakis, a green t-shirt, and the silver watch I'd gifted him for his birthday, its face catching the sunlight. His leather sneakers tapped softly to the rhythm of the forest's bird calls, a subtle expression of his deep affinity for nature, his presence a steady complement to my own.

We arrived at the Puerta Calakmul Hotel around 4:00 p.m., the humid air enveloping us as we stepped out, stretching stiff limbs after the long drive. Arturo's car disappeared down the road, his farewell wave lingering in the dust. The hotel grounds, familiar from a dozen prior visits, felt like a homecoming, their lush surroundings a testament to the forest's dominance. Daniel pointed out red-lored Amazon parrots perched in nearby trees, their crimson foreheads vivid, his eyes alight with delight at the natural spectacle, a joy we shared.

The hotel's design captivated, its wooden bungalows integrated into the tropical forest, each a private haven linked by dirt pathways to the office and restaurant. The architecture honored the environment, the forest's canopy framing the structures like a living embrace. We checked in, our footsteps muffled on the path, the anticipation of meeting our team blending with the forest's vibrant sounds, a prelude to the discoveries awaiting us at Huntuunich.

Our bungalow emerged along the pathway, nestled among Honduras mahogany, ceiba, and strangler fig trees, their dense foliage alive with activity. A spider monkey swung on a branch near the entrance, its chatter mingling with a keel-billed toucan's call, its rainbow beak a striking contrast to the green. A grey hawk's cry sounded faintly, the forest's sounds overwhelming up close, a chorus of life that defied cataloging. The bungalow's porch, with its chairs and hammock, offered a place to pause, though the site's mysteries urged us forward.

Inside, screened walls replaced windows, wooden blinds providing privacy, the forest's sounds—parrots' squawks, monkeys' hoots—filtered through, a constant presence. A mural of scarlet macaws, their feathers vibrant, adorned the wall above the king-size bed, its ruby bedspread accented by urticaria leaves. The thatched ceiling, supported by wooden beams, housed a ceiling fan and mosquito net, the only defenses against the heat, while a modern bathroom with a tiled shower offered comfort. We placed our luggage by the left screen, the forest's rhythm a quiet backdrop, our brief respite a moment to gather strength for the work ahead.

With an hour before our team's arrival, Daniel and I set out to explore the hotel's trails, the main pathway branching into narrow tracks winding through the forest. Butterflies danced in the sunlight, their wings flashing iridescent hues, while an agouti scurried across our path, its small form vanishing into the underbrush. One trail promised sightings of howler monkeys, their deep roars echoing faintly, mingling with the crackle of leaves beneath our feet. Daniel's hand clasped mine, his touch warm, his hazel eyes scanning the canopy, a shared curiosity driving us deeper into the jungle's embrace.

The humidity pressed against us, a heavy warmth that prickled my nostrils, my skin growing clammy within minutes. Mosquitoes buzzed relentlessly, their bites a constant irritation, and I brushed them away, wary of hidden dangers like tarantulas or snakes coiled in the shadows. The forest demanded constant awareness, its beauty intertwined with its challenges, yet the prospect of Huntuunich's ruins fueled my resolve, each step a preparation for the archaeological work ahead, the site's secrets waiting to be uncovered.

Daniel glanced at his watch, noting 4:50 p.m., and quickened his pace, our 5:00 p.m. meeting at the restaurant drawing near. My stomach rumbled as the thought of taco salads with crisp lettuce and tangy salsa sharpened my hunger. We turned back, the forest's sounds swelling as dusk approached, bats stirring in a nearby cave, their wings a soft flutter through the trees. The restaurant's silhouette emerged, its thatched roof a beacon, the meeting a pivotal moment that would set the course for our time at Huntuunich.

We couldn't have known then how profoundly that meeting would alter our lives. Our previous Calakmul trips, focused on academic research, had been straightforward, the ruins a familiar ground for exploration. Yet, as we neared the restaurant, a subtle unease took root, a premonition that Huntuunich held complexities beyond its stone structures—perhaps whispers of the Kukulkan sect or Maria's eventual betrayal. The experiences ahead, both exhilarating and challenging, would reshape my perspective, leaving a lasting imprint on my heart.

The hotel's restaurant stood invitingly, its leaf-shaped tables arranged beneath a high, thatched ceiling, large windows framing the pond, now reflecting the twilight's deepening colors. The air carried the scent of grilled corn and fresh herbs, a contrast to the forest's earthy aroma, the space alive with the promise of connection. We paused at the entrance, scanning for familiar faces, the team's expertise a foundation for unraveling Huntuunich's history, their presence a bridge to the site's past.

The forest's influence lingered, its sounds a constant undercurrent as we stood on the restaurant's threshold. The ruins, concealed by centuries of growth, held stories of a civilization lost to time, their glyphs a code Maria would help us read. Dr. McAdoo's leadership, combined with the team's diverse skills, gave the project weight, but the undercurrents of what lay ahead—intrigue, personal conflicts—cast a faint shadow, one I sensed but couldn't yet articulate.

Our earlier walk had been rich with detail, the spider monkey's playful antics and the toucan's vivid beak etching themselves into memory. The hawk's distant call, the forest's overwhelming chorus, had been a reminder of the jungle's vitality, a force that both welcomed and tested us. Daniel's hand in mine, his appreciation for the natural world evident in his attentive gaze, had steadied me, a partnership that would carry us through the challenges ahead.

The bungalow's features—the macaws' vibrant mural, the ruby bedspread's bold hue, the mosquito net's gentle drape—remained clear, a temporary refuge before the campsite's demands. The forest's sounds, permeating the screens, had been a vivid backdrop, their intensity a testament to the wildness surrounding us. As we approached the restaurant, the meeting's significance grew, the team's collective knowledge a tool to probe Huntuunich's depths, its mysteries poised to reveal themselves.

My hunger for the taco salads intensified, their anticipated flavors a small comfort amidst the project's uncertainties. The restaurant's warmth, its windows catching the last light, felt like a gateway, the meeting a step into uncharted territory. Dr. McAdoo's guidance, Maria's linguistic skills, and the team's shared purpose would anchor us, yet the sect's influence and Maria's betrayal, though still hidden, loomed like a distant threat, their presence felt in the forest's restless hum.

Looking back, that January afternoon was a turning point; Huntuunich's ruins a catalyst for profound change. The drive's tranquility, the hotel's unique charm, and the forest's vivid life were a prelude to trials and discoveries that would define us. The memories, both cherished and challenging, remain vivid, each moment a piece of a journey that transformed me, its lessons enduring in my heart.

The forest's rhythm, the bungalow's quiet comfort, and Daniel's unwavering presence framed that day, each element a facet of a larger narrative. Huntuunich's glyphs, the sect's secrets, and the betrayals to come would test my resilience. Still, in that moment, only the meeting's promise and the ruins' allure propelled me forward, a path into the unknown that would redefine our lives.

As we entered the restaurant, the faint murmur of voices signaling our team's arrival, a quiet determination settled within me. Huntuunich's history, intertwined with Calakmul's legacy, awaited our exploration, its story ready to unfold through our efforts, its shadows—sect, betrayal, time's mysteries—yet to emerge fully, but already echoing in the forest's timeless song.

CHAPTER 2

The restaurant at Puerta Calakmul Hotel enveloped us in rustic elegance, its tables carved like giant leaves glowing under the soft light of woven lanterns, their curves echoing the tropical forest's organic sprawl. Floor-to-ceiling windows framed a small pond, its surface shimmering with the late afternoon sun, fringed by strangler figs and ceiba trees, their reflections dancing in the water. The thatched, vaulted roof soared above, lending an airy grandeur. The scent of fresh tortillas and citrus blooms wafted through, a sanctuary after our journey from Belize.

We stepped inside, my gladiator sandals whispering on the wooden floor, and spotted Dr. McAdoo at a back table by the windows, a woman beside him. He was in his mid-forties, his salt-and-pepper hair and greying beard framed an oblong face, and his aqua-blue eyes reflected the pond's water. His alabaster complexion, marked by age spots, contrasted with the tan safari vest he wore over a white long-sleeve shirt and khaki pants. His chubby frame exuded a quiet authority. He saw us, his smile broad, and rose, beckoning us over, the forest's distant hum a soft accompaniment to the scene.

Dr. McAdoo settled into the left aisle seat, facing away from the window, with the woman to his right. I took the seat opposite her. Daniel sat across from Dr. McAdoo, the leaf-shaped table's eight chairs spacious yet intimate.

"Clara, Daniel," he said, his Cambridge accent warm, "this is Maria Lopez, an archaeologist with the Mexican government."

Maria was in her late twenties, with a heart-shaped face, chestnut-brown eyes, a hazelnut complexion, and long black hair cascading straight over her shoulders. Her purple silk blouse, dark jeans, and silver sandals were refined. She wore an opal ring and a gleaming abalone butterfly bracelet, her Mayan ancestry a silent bond with mine.

A sound at the entrance drew our gaze—three newcomers approached, their footsteps echoing. Dr. McAdoo stood again, his enthusiasm palpable, and greeted them with a beaming smile. "Everyone," he announced, "meet Evelyn Irving, our anthropology and archaeobotany specialist."

Evelyn, in her early forties, radiated whimsy, her auburn hair tucked under a tan sun hat and her floral shirt vibrant beneath a safari vest. His gaze shifted to the second woman, his blue eyes sparkling, his hand trembling slightly as he shook hers. "Samantha Vasques, our archaeozoologist," he said, his voice fervent.

He turned to the man, his tone brisker. "And Dr. Archer, our GIS director and archaeometry specialist." Dr. Archer's presence commanded attention, his partial heterochromia—green fading to blue—striking. Daniel rose, his cocoa skin tone warm in the light, and extended a hand.

"I am Daniel Bennett, and this is my wife, Clara," he said, his voice steady. "We focus on architecture, art history, and ethnoarchaeology." His chestnut hair caught the light, his silver watch, my gift, glinting, anchoring our shared purpose.

Dr. McAdoo nodded, gesturing to Maria. "Maria will work with Clara and Daniel, translating glyphs as our Mayan linguist and epigrapher." Her warm smile, her opal ring catching the light, promised collaboration. Dr. Archer's gaze settled on me, his voice measured.

"You're Belizean, per the roster," he said. "I've excavated there—gorgeous beaches, turquoise waters, coral reefs ideal for diving." His olive skin and light brown hair with golden highlights framed a stern face, a flicker of curiosity softening his tone.

"I am," I replied, my amber eyes meeting his. "Daniel and I met at Galen University in San Ignacio, where we work for the government. I'm from San Pedro on Ambergris Caye—my parents run a restaurant on Main Street."

Memories of San Pedro's salty breeze flickered through my mind, a contrast to the forest's humid breath beyond the windows.

Evelyn chimed in, her honey-brown eyes bright. "I'm from Greenwich, London," she said cheerfully. "Dr. Archer, where are you from?" Her tan cargo pants and leather boots suited the jungle, I thought, and I liked her attitude.

Dr. Archer's gaze flicked to her, a faint smirk curling his lips. "Panama City, Panama," he said, his tone guarded.

Evelyn pressed, her curiosity evident. "What do you do there?" she asked, her heart-shaped face tilted.

"I'm a government archaeologist," he replied, "temporarily reassigned to Mexico for this project, like many of you." He was evasive, a hint of secrecy perhaps tied to Huntuunich's mysteries. I couldn't shake thoughts about the shadow of the Kukulkan sect.

Evelyn's smile widened, her alabaster complexion glowing. She was 5'5" and of average weight, her warmth countering Dr. Archer's sternness. Her floral shirt was a welcome burst of color. Dr. Archer was in his early thirties and tall, 6'2", with an athletic build, an aquiline nose, and thin lips framing a face both handsome and serious, his heterochromia mesmerizing. His tan khakis and blue button-down shirt were crisp. He had an enigmatic demeanor, and I sensed a quiet tension underlying the team's budding camaraderie.

Dr. McAdoo cleared his throat, motioning for us to sit. "Let's review the project," he said, his voice steadying. "Dr. Archer's team has cleared much of Huntuunich's ceremonial center and surrounding structures, setting a datum point for elevation measurements. The site is vast, but dense vegetation slows clearing to protect material culture." His fingers tapped the table, a trace of anxiety belying his calm, the pond's darkening reflection a backdrop to his words.

He continued, his eyes sweeping the group. "More specialists will join us soon. We're in the survey's early phase, and the NIAH has named the site Huntuunich—'alone rock' in Mayan, likely its original name per glyph references. Tomorrow, we airlift to the site via helicopter, as Calakmul's reserve forbids roads." His words ignited excitement, Huntuunich's glyphs a puzzle awaiting Maria's expertise, the ruins a canvas for discovery.

He concluded, his tone measured, "If Mexico opens Huntuunich to tourists, infrastructure may follow, but for now, we map its layout and history. Our base camp, a quarter-mile north of the ceremonial center, uses a clearing from old ranching days, partly overgrown but accessible." He seemed suddenly distracted, his gaze flickering to the pond, a quiet tension hinting at unspoken concerns.

Evelyn's smile turned to Daniel and me, her cheer a warm light. "How did you join this project?" she asked, her voice lilting.

"The NIAH invited us, through Dr. McAdoo," I said, "after our roles in Belize's government archaeology." Evelyn nodded, sharing her Oxford professorship, her transfer to Huntuunich unexpected but a "chance of a lifetime" for a new Mayan site. Her warmth contrasted Samantha's silence. She was tall, about 5'9", with butterscotch blonde hair tied with a gold clip, distant emerald eyes, a storm brewing beneath her poise.

Samantha's presence was captivating. She had an oval face with a flawless olive complexion, her small, upturned nose framed by French-manicured nails, impractical for fieldwork's demands. She wore a multicolored tank top, black flowing skirt, and gold designer sandals, with glinting beaded bracelets and a necklace. However, her agitation was palpable. Catching my glance, I offered a smile, but her glare, sharp and cold, sent a chill through me.

Scents wafting through the restaurant—grilled peppers, fresh salsa—stirred my hunger, the pond now a dark mirror as dusk fell. "Shall we order?" I suggested, my voice cutting through the chatter. Daniel and I chose taco salads, their crisp greens and tangy salsa a delight, paired with a fruit juice of mango, pineapple, banana, strawberry, and kiwi. It was so wonderfully sweet we ordered seconds. The meal grounded us, the leaf-shaped table a stage for new bonds and quiet doubts.

Maria and Evelyn's conversation flowed, Maria's insights on Mayan glyphs sparking anticipation, Evelyn's Oxford anecdotes charming. Dr. McAdoo's distraction deepened, his fingers drumming. His clear anxiety contrasted starkly with his usual calm.

As darkness shrouded the pond, exhaustion settled in, and Daniel and I excused ourselves, the forest's nocturnal hum guiding us to our bungalow.

A tropical chorus pierced the bungalow's screens, parrots and monkeys heralding sunrise before 7:00 a.m., a majestic yet intrusive alarm. I savored the comfort of the bed, knowing that it was a luxury we wouldn't have on the trail. "Sleeping bags await," I murmured, rising from bed, my ginger hair tangled. The call of the forest was both thrilling and daunting, Huntuunich's ruins a beckoning mystery.

The delicious aroma of coffee drew us to the restaurant, where we were met with a continental spread of pastries, fruits, eggs, sausage, and waffles. I chose a banana, an orange, and chai tea, savoring the perishables, knowing campsite supplies would be more sparse. Daniel indulged in eggs, sausage, waffles, and tea. He was clearly excited, his love for the outdoors bubbling to the surface. His cocoa skin was warm in the morning light, his hazel eyes bright with purpose.

We grabbed fruit for the campsite as the team assembled. Samantha was conspicuously absent. Dr. McAdoo announced a 10:00 a.m. departure, his voice steady but eyes distant. My anticipation surged despite my dread of months in tents and sleeping on hard ground. I wore an old white peasant blouse with blue embroidery, jeans, and hiking boots, my hair pulled back in a ponytail secured with a red leather barrette. It featured Mayan glyphs that spelled out "Clara," a gift from Daniel.

Daniel's long-sleeve shirt and cargo pants matched the team's practical attire. The scent of sunscreen and bug spray lingered in the air, but I skipped the greasy spray, trusting the openness of the clearing would protect me. We returned to the bungalow to gather our gear. Daniel went to the restaurant to get Wi-Fi and check his email. Alone for a moment, I flicked through TV channels, finding nothing, the forest's hum providing a restless backdrop to my thoughts.

Boredom nudged me to join Daniel, but a brochure on the writing desk stopped me. "Where did this come from?" I wondered. It wasn't there yesterday. It depicted a man on a rope bridge above the forest, advertising for a hotel near Huntuunich. Bungalows on stilts linked by bridges. The copy said it offered an "explorer experience" for Calakmul tourism. Designed by Juan Cortez, it seemed impossible that such a place could exist in a protected reserve, but I tucked it into my tote bag, a nagging sense that it was important somehow. Maybe a clue to the sect's schemes?

In the restaurant, Daniel sat by the windows with his laptop open, a pastry crumb on his lip. He smiled at me, his hazel eyes warm, the pond a bright mirror in the morning light. I headed for the breakfast table, eyeing the glass pitchers of juice, when Samantha's voice sliced through, sharp and mocking. "Kind of tacky, don't you think?" she said, nodding at my barrette. Her gold-clipped hair framed her smug smirk, her gold sandals glinting in the sunlight.

"Excuse me?" I said, heat rising at the unexpected insult.

"The barrette," she clarified, her emerald eyes narrowing, her tone dripping with disdain.

Shock mingled with embarrassment—Daniel was watching, his brow furrowing. "No worse than your artificial nails," I retorted, my voice steady, noting her impractical manicure. Her smirk twisted into a scowl, and she stormed off, muttering under her breath, her skirt swishing, the air thick with her hostility.

Daniel's gaze followed me as I grabbed some orange juice. "What was that about?" he asked gently as I plopped down.

"I'm not sure," I said, sipping the juice, "but it's more than petty rivalry." He nodded, returning to his emails, advising me to ignore Samantha, but a knot formed in my gut. I couldn't get her glare out of my mind. And what of the brochure and its seemingly impossible promise? Huntuunich's secrets loomed ever larger.

CHAPTER 3

*T*he restaurant's warmth lingered as Daniel and I sat amidst the morning's bustle, the aroma of coffee and fresh fruit mingling with the tropical forest's distant hum filtering through the open windows. At 9:45 a.m., Daniel glanced at his silver watch, its face catching the light, and murmured, "We should go." He closed his laptop with a quiet snap, his hazel eyes meeting mine, a shared anticipation for Huntuunich's ruins. We rose, my tote bag slung over my shoulder, its weight a reminder of the brochure's enigma, Juan Cortez's impossible hotel a puzzle yet to unravel.

We stepped onto the dirt pathway, the crunch of fallen leaves under my hiking boots blending with the forest's chorus—parrots' screeches, monkeys' chatter, a grey hawk's cry piercing the humid air. Over the cacophony, a low thrum emerged, helicopters approaching, their rhythmic pulse quickening my heart. The path wound through Honduras mahogany and ceiba trees, their canopies alive with life, the air thick with the scent of damp earth and blooming orchids, Huntuunich's call growing louder with each step.

In the parking lot, a clearing buzzed with activity, two helicopters' propellers slowing, stirring dust and leaves in a whirlwind. Maria and Evelyn approached from the hotel's path, their luggage trailing, Maria's black hair gleaming, and Evelyn's auburn locks tucked under her sun hat.

Dr. Archer strode leisurely from the office, his 6'2" frame imposing, his green-blue eyes scanning us with a stern glint.

"You four go first," he said, his voice clipped, gesturing to the helicopters. "We'll follow." Daniel and I chose the right one, while Maria and Evelyn chose the left; the team's division marked a quiet prelude to the site's mysteries.

We boarded our helicopter, where the pilot stowed our luggage with practiced ease. Daniel took the front passenger seat beside him, his lean frame relaxed, while I settled in the back, caddy-corner to Daniel, my tote bag clutched tightly. Our bags filled the seat beside me, their weight grounding me as the engine roared to life. Takeoff sent adrenaline surging. The helicopter's rumble was deafening, the shaking rattling my nerves. I loathed flying, especially in helicopters, their noise and wind amplifying my unease, but Daniel's grin and evident love for flight steadied me.

"Almost there," he called, turning to flash a reassuring smile, his chestnut hair ruffled by the cabin's draft. I nodded, gripping my seat, my amber eyes fixed on the window. The tropical forest unfolded below, a verdant tapestry blanketing hills and valleys, its vastness humbling. I imagined Cyrus Lundell's awe in 1931, rediscovering Calakmul from the air, its ruins hidden beneath the canopy. Our site, 31 miles northeast of Calakmul, lay 68 miles from the Puerta Calakmul Hotel, its remoteness a shield until now.

The helicopter shuddered violently at full altitude, the wind's turbulence jolting me. "I'll be glad to land," I muttered, my heart racing. The forest's green sea was a dizzying blur. Daniel's calm presence, his gaze on the horizon, eased my fear, Huntuunich's promise outweighing the flight's discomfort. The clearing emerged, a grassy expanse west of a massive temple, its stone peak piercing the forest's overgrowth, an eerie silhouette against the vibrant jungle.

My breath caught, not with wonder but unease, the temple's decay a haunting scene, a ghost of Huntuunich's past rather than the marvel I'd expected. The four-acre field, carved by ranchers before the reserve's protection, had been partly reclaimed by forest, its edges blurring into the jungle. We landed north of the temple, the pilot's steady hand a relief. The solidity of the ground was a welcome embrace after the flight's chaos.

Daniel and I hauled our luggage to a central pile of camping gear, with smaller stacks labeled for each team member; the canvas and metal presented a stark contrast to the forest's organic sprawl. We moved our supplies 50 feet south, waiting for the others before erecting tents—one for sleeping, another for storage and office use. The clearing's openness felt liberating but exposed, the temple's shadow looming. Huntuunich's secrets lay just beyond the trees.

Helicopters returned, their thrum heralding Maria and Evelyn's arrival. Maria stepped out first, her hazelnut complexion glowing, followed by Evelyn, her whimsical air undimmed by the journey. They dragged their luggage to the pile, retrieved their camping gear, and placed their bags behind our tent before returning for more. The second helicopter brought Dr. McAdoo, Samantha, and Dr. Archer, their figures emerging against the forest's green. The team was now complete.

Dr. Archer approached unnoticed, his presence startling as Dr. McAdoo's voice cut through. "Fifteen minutes, we tour the site," he announced, his aqua eyes scanning us. "Then we set up camp." I grabbed two water bottles from our gear, their cool plastic somehow reassuring, along with gloves, a compass, and machetes. My anticipation surged, tempered by the temple's eerie aura, a whisper of Huntuunich's hidden truths.

We moved toward the forest's entrance, the clearing's grass yielding to dense undergrowth. Dr. Archer fell in step, his site map in hand, his voice low. "I'd like your first impressions," he said, his gaze piercing. "Architecture, art history—what do you see?" His curiosity softened his sternness. The map's coordinates hinted at structure despite the jungle's chaos. I nodded, the machete's handle firm in my grip, ready to uncover Huntuunich's past.

Parrots screeched in the distance, their vibrant calls echoing as we crossed the clearing. Howler monkeys roared above, their silhouettes darting through the canopy, the trail's entrance a gateway to the forest's heart. A coati scampered at the path's edge, its raccoon-like form fleeting. The pulse of the forest seemed to quicken with each step, the humidity a warm breath against my skin.

Bug spray helped combat the relentless mosquitoes and flies, but their bites remained a constant irritation, even with my long-sleeve blouse. A toucan soared overhead, its beak a vivid arc, and a rustling revealed a

Yucatan brown brocket deer with big ears. Ocellated turkeys darted through the undergrowth, their iridescent feathers flashing, the forest a living entity, its dirt-and-flower scent and humid exhale enveloping us, speaking through animal calls and rustling leaves.

The trail was well cleared, requiring little use of machetes, although roots and branches demanded caution to avoid tripping. Basilisk lizards skittered past, along with an agouti staring boldly, its gaze unnerving. Ahead, the pyramid temple's stone base loomed through the trees, its grandeur both thrilling and foreboding.

I froze, the temple's stone base towering in front of us, its grand staircase a marvel of Mayan craftsmanship unveiled through the forest's veil. Glyphs and relief sculptures adorned the risers, their chiseled forms vivid despite centuries of wear, a faint red paint clinging to the carvings, hinting at Huntuunich's vibrant past. The reliefs, sculpted to stand proud from the stone, cast shadows that danced in the dappled light, their three-dimensional grace a testament to ancient artistry.

The pyramid, rising some 90 feet, was modest compared to grander Mayan structures, its nine layers marking it as a burial temple, a portal to the underworld's nine gods. Its height had shielded it from discovery, the overgrown forest a perfect cloak until now. Each layer narrowed, crowned by a roof comb, its silhouette eerie against the jungle's green, the temple's decay was both haunting and magnetic, stirring images of secrets tied to the Kukulkan sect.

Dr. Archer guided us to the ceremonial center, a sprawling plaza shaped by Huntuunich's rugged geology. The layout was haphazard yet deliberate. Monumental structures ringed the open space—pyramid temples, royal palaces, religious and government buildings—linked by causeways, with a ball court to the south. Stelae and altars dotted the center, their friezes depicting divine rulers, each katun's 20-year cycle etched to affirm their reign. Huntuunich's history was carved in stone.

He detailed the surveyed layout: the burial pyramid to the north, religious pyramids facing east and west, rows of stelae before them, and the ball court anchoring the plaza's south. Yet the forest's overgrowth hid these, visibility limited to just ten feet. The path ended abruptly south of the burial temple. "Records claim these are cleared," I whispered to Daniel, his nod mirroring my doubt. The discrepancy was a puzzle, hinting at oversight or perhaps some hidden intent; could it be the sect's influence?

We circled the temple's 200-foot-square base, its 15-foot-wide staircase facing south. The risers were covered with intricate glyphs, their reliefs a narrative of kings and conquests. Limestone stucco, once smooth, was weathered and eroded by time, with plants clinging to the stone, their roots invasive, scaling nearly to the roof comb. The overgrowth, a living shroud, had concealed Huntuunich for centuries. This reemergence was a fragile gift.

Daniel and I ascended the staircase, its narrow, steep steps treacherous without railings. My boots slipped on mossy stone. Halfway up, I paused, glancing back, the forest's dense canopy obscuring all but green, an impenetrable veil. Chisel marks marred the steps, evidence of a past search for a royal tomb—a Mayan practice of hiding burials within staircases, sealed by remodeled stone. The glyphs here spoke of a great king, their meaning elusive to my limited knowledge.

"My glyphs are rusty," I admitted to Daniel.

He smiled encouragingly, "Maria will decode them." The carvings hinted at Huntuunich's role in the Tikal–Calakmul rivalry, a vassal breaking free, its independence etched in stone. Tomorrow, with Maria's expertise, we'll learn more, unraveling Huntuunich's past.

Back at the campsite, the scent of rice and beans wafted sensuously. I realized how hungry I was after all the hours spent exploring. Evelyn and Maria sat on Evelyn's tent porch, its red-and-white floral chairs a splash of color, the tent erected in our absence. Her tent stood behind ours, with Maria's beyond our planned office tent to the left, both facing south. Dr. Archer headed to his gear, his tent to our right.

Evelyn waved us over, her smile warm. "I set up your tent," she said, her auburn hair catching the light. "You were with Archer." We thanked her, fetching our camp chairs to join them, the grass cool beneath my boots. Dr. McAdoo, cooking nearby, served us bowls of rice and beans, their warmth comforting, the spice a jolt to my senses.

"How was it?" he asked, his aqua eyes curious.

"Fantastic," I said, spooning the beans, "but we lost track of time."

Maria's voice cut in, surprised. "Lunch? It's past five." Her chestnut eyes widened, and I laughed, the temple's allure having stolen the day. I asked Dr. McAdoo for the site records, and he pointed to a black-lidded tote by his tents—one for sleeping, one an office—his organization served as an anchor amidst the chaos of the camp.

After dinner, I reviewed the records, which confirmed that the tote's contents had cleared structures, yet the site's overgrowth told a different story. The discrepancy nagged at me. Returning, I overheard Samantha and Dr. McAdoo arguing near the clearing's western edge, their voices faint but heated. She was angry, and his tone was restrained. The distance muffled the details, but the intensity was obvious, a rift hinting at tensions tied to Huntuunich's secrets—perhaps even Maria's future betrayal.

Daniel and I erected our second tent, its tan canvas matching the others, mesh porches and windows offering scant protection from the forest's hum. Dusk settled, the wind rustling the canvas, mosquitoes buzzing outside, the forest's nocturnal chorus subdued. Exhaustion washed over me. Tomorrow's glyph work with Maria promised answers, but the argument and site records left me feeling uneasy.

Sleep came fitfully. Daniel's steady breathing helped comfort me, and I fell into slumber. A sudden sound—quick footsteps racing past, heading south to the site—jolted us awake. The bathrooms lay north, making the direction illogical, the late hour ominous. "Who's that?" I whispered, fear gripping me, the footsteps fading into the night. Daniel's silence mirrored my dread. The hum of the forest had turned to menace.

I lay still, my heart pounding, willing sleep to return, but the echo of those footsteps lingered, a harbinger of Huntuunich's hidden truths. The glyphs, the sect's shadow, and Maria's betrayal ran through my mind. Clinging to Daniel's warmth, I tried to ignore the bad feelings arising in me. Huntuunich's call was both thrilling and perilous, but secrets were waiting to unravel.

CHAPTER 4

*M*orning sunlight pierced the tent's mesh, bathing the interior in a soft golden glow, while the jungle's lively chorus of squawking parrots, chattering monkeys, and humming insects awakened my senses. I slipped into tan cargo pants, their lightweight cotton smooth against my cinnamon skin, and a deep purple long-sleeve shirt, its vibrant hue a subtle rebellion against the rising heat. My sturdy hiking boots, scuffed from prior treks, anchored me to the day's purpose, and I gathered my ginger hair into a ponytail, its gentle motion reflecting the anticipation surging within me. Stepping outside, I breathed in the humid air, rich with the scent of damp soil and distant orchid blooms, a calming presence that readied me for Huntuunich's ancient secrets.

Daniel had risen earlier and was seated in a multicolored camp chair in front of our tent. He was dressed in grey cargo pants and a royal blue long-sleeve shirt, a grey bucket hat shielding his hazel eyes. His tired smile, shadowed by the memory of last night's mysterious footsteps, offered quiet reassurance, his steady demeanor grounding me in the dawn's gentle warmth. The campsite stirred with subtle activity, its canvas tents dotting the clearing. Their elongated shadows merged with the jungle's verdant edge, a reminder of the challenges awaiting us in this remote wilderness.

We strolled toward the kitchen area, located northeast of the campsite, where a charcoal grill and camping stove rested on a folding table, forming the heart of our rustic operations. A pipe spigot, connected to a well dug before our arrival, shimmered in the morning light, its cool stream a brief respite from the heat. The food storage tent, its canvas walls taut, stood nearby, safeguarding our provisions and symbolizing our endurance in the relentless jungle environment. Each element of the camp sharpened my focus, preparing me for the archaeological work ahead.

For breakfast, we opened a can of room-temperature fruit juice and unwrapped granola bars, their citrus zest and nutty flavor sharp against the morning's humidity. The simple meal evoked last night's dessert, when we savored the hotel's fresh fruit in folding chairs beneath the warm embrace of dusk, a fleeting indulgence now replaced by necessity. The juice's tang lingered on my tongue, a modest comfort that sustained my energy for the day's demands, anchoring my resolve.

I visited the restroom facility, its tiled sinks and twin toilet-shower stalls, an unexpected touch of modernity here in the wild. Brushing my teeth, I caught my reflection in the mirror. My amber eyes were alight with determination. The cool water splashing my face offered a refreshing pause. The facility's practicality balanced the jungle's rawness, reinforcing our structured mission to uncover Huntuunich's historical truths, each moment a step toward discovery.

Maria stood near our tent as I returned, her warm smile easing my tension. She was wearing a dark green long-sleeve shirt and light brown cargo pants, well-suited for the day's labor. A light purple backpack hung over her shoulder, and her ponytail swayed with quiet confidence. I grabbed my blue backpack, which was filled with canned fruit, granola bars, and bottled water, its familiar weight a reminder of the jungle's challenges. The acrid scent of sunscreen clung to our skin, a necessary defense against the sun's fierce rays, preparing us for the trek to the temple site.

At the temple, we unpacked sketchbooks, paperwork, cameras, and tape measures from an aluminum clipboard, their cool metal reassuring in my hands. Maria ascended the staircase, her eyes tracing the weathered glyphs and friezes, their faint red paint a whisper of ancient artistry. Daniel adjusted his camera, capturing the carvings' intricate details, while I examined the staircase for signs of a hidden burial entrance. A curious lizard watched me with beady eyes, its small form a spark of life against the stone's silence.

The sun's heat intensified. Sweat soaked my shirt, the jungle's humidity wrapping around me like a heavy cloak. We paused for lunch, the canned fruit's sweetness a soothing relief, its coolness easing the day's strain. Maria shared tales of her Mexico City upbringing. She told us of her nurse mother and professor father, painting a vivid picture. Somehow her story made me feel closer to her. Daniel spoke of his schoolteacher mother and journalist father, and I mentioned my great-grandmother Clara, half British and half Greek, whose name, meaning "clear," connected me to my heritage.

We climbed to the temple's rooftop comb, a compact structure atop the pyramid, its murals depicting ancient kings in striking detail. We moved toward the single square door with a blend of excitement and caution. It was seven feet tall and wide, its stucco remarkably intact compared to the pyramid's eroded base. The comb's elevated perch revealed the shocking expanse of the jungle canopy, its immensity both humbling and inspiring.

The comb's weathered stone circle, soaring thirty feet, grabbed our attention. What was its purpose? Perhaps a royal headdress, or was it a sacred symbol? Although decay obscured its original design, each crack in the stone ignited my curiosity, offering clues to Huntuunich's storied past. Maria's steady voice, noting the circle's precise alignment, anchored our theories, her insight a reminder of our collective goal to piece together the site's historical narrative.

Inside the comb's fourteen-foot-square room, faded murals adorned the bare walls, their chipped paint revealing glimpses of ancient life. Maria translated the glyphs with calm precision, her enthusiasm infectious as she traced the lineage of twelve life-sized kings on the left wall, their ornate headdresses commanding reverence. The twelfth king stood out, his story etched in stone, a testament to Huntuunich's enduring pride.

The seventh century saw Calakmul's Kaan Dynasty dominate, its snake emblem a symbol of authority, giving way by A.D. 800 to a bat emblem, signaling a shift in regional power. The back wall depicted King Night Eagle's victory over Calakmul, wearing a vivid feathered headdress and leopard-skin sash. His success represented a bold claim of Huntuunich's strength. Each glyph, meticulously carved, drew me into the region's intricate history, a complex tapestry of alliances and conflicts.

In A.D. 734, Quiriguá's rebellion against Copan, a Tikal vassal, with Calakmul's support, echoed Huntuunich's own defiance of Mayan elites. Night Eagle, rejecting his brothers Sun Jaguar and Snake Smoke, aligned with Calakmul's waning influence, shaping the site's independence. The glyphs told a rich narrative, filled with tales of conflict, deepening my understanding of Huntuunich's role in the Mayan world—a legacy we were only beginning to unravel.

The right wall portrayed Night Eagle and his peasant wife, Xochitl, in a bustling marketplace, her reddish-orange huipil striking against the stone. Influenced by Calakmul's artistic style, the scene featured woven baskets and lively crowds, yet it bore Huntuunich's unique architectural flourishes. Xochitl's rare depiction as a commoner highlighted Night Eagle's unconventional reign. It resonated with me as a reflection of the site's distinct identity, a marker of its singular character.

A missing structure, possibly an altar or zoomorph, left a space in the room, its absence a compelling riddle. Beneath the stucco, a faint, hidden painting hinted at undiscovered secrets, its colors barely discernible in the dim light. At the same time, the oppressive heat weighed heavily on me. I was dehydrated due to the relentless humidity, yet the room's mysteries held my focus, each clue a step closer to illuminating Huntuunich's heritage.

When we returned to camp, we all drank greedily from water bottles in the kitchen tent, its canvas shade a welcome refuge from the day's exertions. Evelyn joined us; her botanical studies suggested a sprawling site. However, she expressed unease, saying she felt like we were being watched, casting a subtle shadow over our conversation. Dr. Archer's guitar strumming and McAdoo's rare laughter helped break the mood, introducing some brief levity to the evening. Maria's dancing and Daniel's playful tug drew me into the moment, although Samantha's absence lingered. Despite the smiles, a quiet tension lurked beneath our fragile camaraderie, reminding us of the complex social undercurrents in our camp.

CHAPTER 5

The next morning, we gathered at the boat to head to Rosalina's Kitchen at the river stop, following the trail Miguel had taken the previous day. I dressed in a light blue T-shirt adorned with vibrant orange flowers, its cotton soft against my cinnamon skin, paired with snug jeans and gladiator sandals. My silver azalea necklace gleamed, and my turquoise bangle, etched with decorative Mayan glyphs, caught the sunlight. With my ginger hair swept into a bun, I felt refreshed, the chance to dress up lifting my spirits, offering a brief escape from Huntuunich's demanding routine.

Daniel walked beside me, his red T-shirt bright against his worn jeans, his silver watch glinting with each step, his steady presence a quiet comfort. Mosquitoes and gnats swarmed relentlessly, their bites barely dulled by the sharply scented bug spray, a constant irritation in the humid air. The project's initial allure had faded, and the harsh realities of our rugged camp life were settling in. Yet this trip to the river stop promised solace, a momentary reprieve from our daily challenges.

Samantha arrived last, her side braid shining, her yellow sundress with blue butterflies flowing gracefully. An oversized straw hat and designer sunglasses shaded her eyes, and her brown thong-toed sandals clicked softly as she walked. Her tan and raspberry-striped tote bag, with braided rope handles, swung heavily, her gold charm bracelet jangling. Her elegance was striking yet somehow out of place, hinting at intentions I couldn't yet decipher. It made me even more curious about her role in this project.

Evelyn's practical outfit—red T-shirt, tan safari vest, bucket hat, cargo pants, and boots—contrasted with Samantha's flair. Her auburn hair peeked from her hat, and her expression was focused and resolute. Her work-ready demeanor anchored my thoughts, a reminder of the dedication driving our efforts at Huntuunich. The team's varied appearances underscored our fraying unity. I knew I'd have to navigate the group dynamics with care.

Maria's casual attire—an old blue T-shirt, jeans, blue flip-flops, and no jewelry—suggested simplicity, her dark eyes scanning the riverbank with quiet intensity. Her understated presence felt deliberate, leaving me curious about her mood. Typically vibrant, she now carried a reserved air. It made me want to observe her actions more closely during this day of leisure.

Dr. McAdoo mirrored Evelyn's diligence, his green T-shirt beneath a tan safari vest, bucket hat, and dark brown cargo pants paired with boots, his stern gaze sweeping the group. His focus on the site's demands stood in contrast to the trip's relaxed intent, a stark reminder of the balance between work and respite. His leadership strengthened my resolve to make the most of this brief escape.

Dr. Archer's laidback style—a white long-sleeve cotton shirt with rolled sleeves, jeans, black flip-flops, and a straw Panama hat—eased the group's tension. His green-blue eyes glittered with anticipation. His relaxed demeanor promised a lighter day, lifting my spirits and offering a rare moment of ease amidst the project's pressures. His presence was a lifeline, bridging our strained team dynamics.

We boarded the utility motorboat, its white hull bobbing on the river's surface. Evelyn and McAdoo settled in the front, Archer and Maria in the middle with Samantha, while Daniel and I took the back, Daniel's hand firm on the steering handle. The engine's roar drowned out the forest's sounds, the river's current pulling us westward. The motion invigorated my sense of purpose, offering a welcome shift from the site's relentless routine.

Evelyn's easy smile and Maria's lively chatter lightened the mood, their voices weaving a thread of camaraderie that felt rare and precious. Samantha's silence contrasted with it. Her gaze was fixed on the river's murky brown surface, her detachment like a quiet warning. The team's laughter, though fleeting, warmed me, a reminder of the connections we could still forge despite the growing strain.

The river, deep and opaque, swirled beneath us, its hidden depths stirring a faint unease in me. Scarlet macaws soared above, their colorful wings bursting against the green canopy. Watching them temporarily distracted me from the river's narrow and precarious twenty-five-foot span. The water's steady flow urged caution, yet the promise of the river stop was also exciting. I was ready for what lay ahead.

Around a sharp bend, cream stucco buildings with thatched roofs emerged, plain yet inviting, marking the river stop's village hub—not Bosque as I had assumed. The Singing Quetzal Hotel, a two-story structure, stood out, its presence at once remarkable and frustrating—why camp in the jungle's heat when such comfort was so near? The sight raised questions about our project's logistics, urging me to seek answers about our camp's austerity.

The left riverbank hosted Rosalina's Kitchen and an open-air market, its three walls bustling with groceries and clothing. Their vibrant displays invited exploration. The right bank held a pharmacy, its faded wooden sign stark, and the hotel, its Spanish-style courtyard blooming with flowers, its arched windows and iron gate exuding charm. The contrast between the village's amenities and our camp's simplicity deepened my curiosity about our choices.

Samantha's deliberate glances at the second floor of the hotel suggested familiarity, and her lack of curiosity about the village seemed odd and suspicious. Her poised demeanor was nothing like the team's shared wonder, hinting at hidden motives. Her intensity stood out amidst the river stop's quiet rhythm. I resolved to remain vigilant as we entered this new place.

Dr. Archer docked at the left pier, the hull scraping softly. The forest's silence was a stark shift from the river's hum. We followed a dirt path to Rosalina's Kitchen, its carved door—etched with jaguars, parrots, and monkeys—gleaming faintly. The artistry of the intricately carved floral pewter handle drew me in, a small delight promising a moment of connection amidst the day's uncertainties.

Inside, the restaurant's cream stucco walls, with exposed brick, radiated warmth, the brown tiled floor cool beneath my sandals. The green-painted wooden chairs, carved with desert scenes—a sleeping man by a cactus for me, a rider on horseback for Daniel, a sunflower for Maria—were delightful, their craftsmanship lifting everyone's mood. Evelyn's enthusiasm for each design was infectious, binding us for a moment in the restaurant's rustic elegance.

Teresita, the waitress, greeted us with a radiant smile, her large brown eyes and red-lipped warmth easing my tension. She was short and slim, with long black hair. She gestured for Samantha to sit first, a courtesy Samantha dismissed, letting others take their places, her reaction deepening my intrigue. Teresita's vibrant presence, her nail polish matching her lipstick, helped make the moment feel more normal.

We settled at a circular booth, McAdoo quickly claiming the seat beside Samantha. His intent was clear, but she rebuffed him with indifference. Teresita distributed menus. Daniel and I ordered taco salads, their fresh tang a delight, while others chose sizzling chicken fajitas. Miguel's boat loan had enabled this escape, a gesture for which I was impossibly grateful.

By three o'clock, Dr. Archer rallied us. We stowed snacks from the market—fruit for me, chips for Daniel—in our bags and returned to our work site, trading our casual clothes for work attire. The jungle's heat was heavy and oppressive, a stark reminder of the comfort we'd just experienced.

Weeks passed, and Daniel and Maria spent time photographing the glyphs. They were focused, excluding me, leaving me feeling isolated. In my boredom, I decided to wander. I reached the temple, finding it silent. The absence of others was unsettling, and I began to feel anxious until the unexpected hum of a boat drew me to the river.

Our motorboat, white with a navy-blue interior, was floating there, its motor hot from recent use. Miguel's uneven paint job marked it ours. It was untethered. *Odd*, I thought. Impulsively, I got in and started it up, heading to the river stop.

The river stop's market was humming with life, shoppers weaving through stalls under the humid sun. I docked the white motorboat at the left pier, its navy-blue interior stark against the murky water. Stepping onto the dirt path, I set out to look for fruit and snacks, but a woman halted me. "Are you an archaeologist from the site?" she asked, her voice warm. I nodded, confirming my role at Huntuunich.

Her smile broadened, radiant and welcoming. She introduced herself as Senora Rios, a woman in her late forties with a round face, light green eyes, and an aquiline nose. Silver streaked her chestnut hair, wavy and long, complementing her beige complexion. At 5'4", her slender frame moved gracefully, her presence rooted in the nearby Mayan ejido community.

Senora Rios wore a vibrant tapestry skirt, colors swirling against a navy-blue background, paired with a striped huipil in navy, red, yellow, and green. She peppered me with questions about Huntuunich—its ruins, its history, and job prospects for Bosque, her home. I answered briefly, my pulse quickening. I needed to return before anyone noticed the boat's absence. This trip was reckless, impulsive.

A boat's hum cut through the chatter, approaching from the east. I turned, spotting Samantha with a handsome, slender Hispanic man in an orange T-shirt and jeans. Their sleek speedboat gleamed, docking smoothly. They entered the Singing Quetzal Hotel's courtyard, settling at a wrought-iron table. They seemed intimate and at ease together. Samantha's emerald eyes never met mine, oblivious to my presence.

Senora Rios caught my stare. "Do you know her?" she asked, delighted. I admitted I knew Samantha, and her face lit up. "So you know Juan Cortiz and Samantha Vasques?" she asked, intrigued, her voice dropping conspiratorially as if sharing a local legend.

"I know Samantha, but who's Juan Cortiz?" I asked, my curiosity sharp.

Senora Rios leaned closer. "He's a developer, famous across the Yucatan for his hotel resorts," she explained. She said he was notorious for his ruthlessness and that he was furious after losing a building permit near Huntuunich. He'd planned a resort beside the ruins, seeking to capitalize on wealthy tourists, but the site's discovery halted the plan for environmental review.

"How can he build in a protected reserve?" I pressed, the jungle's humidity clinging to my skin.

"Cortiz is rich and cunning," Senora Rios replied. She told me he framed his resorts as economic salvation, helping out the government by creating jobs in a region battered by economic decline. Bosque's ejido community saw opportunity, but the forest and ruins hung in the balance.

The name Juan Cortiz struck me like lightning. I suddenly realized it matched the brochure in my bungalow. Panic surged—had someone invaded our room? Why? I masked my alarm, searching for more information. "Samantha's wonderful, isn't she?" I kept my voice steady despite my racing heart.

"Oh, absolutely," Senora Rios beamed. "She rose from a poor Mexico City family, studying cosmetology to work at the peninsula's top salon. She styled the elite, meeting Cortiz through a client's party. Now his girlfriend visits to support his permit fight, staying at the hotel." Samantha was no archaeologist, after all. She had fooled us all, and her absences from the site were now glaringly suspect.

Shock rooted me. Samantha's fieldwork was a sham, where her night-time walks were visits with Cortiz? Could he be the camp's intruder, the one whose steps were echoing in the dark? He sounded dangerous, a threat when spurned. I felt a strong urge to get back to Huntuunich.

I bid Senora Rios farewell, my gladiator sandals crunching the path as I hurried to the boat. I returned it as I had found it, with the motor cooling, and rushed to the temple. Daniel was waiting for me, his hazel eyes blazing. "You wandered off without telling me!" he shouted angrily. "No cell towers here—what if you were hurt?"

"I shouldn't have taken the boat," I admitted, my voice rising. "But I found critical information!" Daniel's anger flared. "Critical? Like facing crocodiles?" he snapped, storming off through the thicket. Maria's pink-and-black backpack was gone, her absence a silent jab—her glyph work with Daniel had excluded me, deepening our rivalry.

Guilt gnawed at me as I grabbed my blue backpack from the temple steps. My impulsiveness had been foolish, but Samantha's deception burned hotter. At camp, I brewed Nescafé in the kitchen, writing a timeline in my journal at the dining table. Cortiz's nighttime visits, likely with Samantha, were aimed at securing the permit. Their footsteps were a threat.

Alone, I slipped into Dr. McAdoo's office tent, where I beheld a scattered mess of papers and folders. Three folding tables groaned under it all. It was out of place, so unlike his usual tight order. Four filing cabinets lined the back wall, one drawer ajar. I sifted through papers on the table. There was another Cortiz resort brochure and a building permit approval form. The sight chilled me.

Opening the cracked drawer, I found a file with a stack of papers. On top was a canceled reservation for Samantha, Dr. McAdoo, and Maria at the Singing Quetzal Hotel, alongside a boat rental slip. Another had details about Dr. McAdoo's NIAH appointment in Mexico City, revealing how Cortiz targeted him. It was Samantha's charm that had swayed him, not credentials.

Another paper listed only Dr. McAdoo and Maria as original NIAH participants, with two more to be approved. Samantha's application was there, but none were found for the others. And then I saw a love letter from Samantha to Dr. McAdoo, penned after a meeting at a Mexico City café, in which she gushed about her "archaeology career." There was a serpent glyph on the folder—perhaps Kukulkan—hinting at deeper secrets. I replaced everything carefully, frustrated and upset, but feeling pity for Dr. McAdoo. His naivety was maddening, but I resolved to unravel this tangled web, no matter the cost.

.

CHAPTER 6

$\mathcal{I}$ slipped out of Dr. McAdoo's office tent, the air heavy with secrets. The jungle's dusk chorus—howler monkeys and parrots —masked my steps. I'd gleaned enough for now, and lingering risked discovery. As I neared my tent, Maria, Samantha, Evelyn, and Dr. McAdoo emerged from the trail, their voices low. Maria's presence startled me; I'd assumed she was at camp, her absence another slight in our quiet rivalry.

The group dispersed, Dr. McAdoo and Evelyn heading to the kitchen to prepare dinner. Tension hung over the camp, sharper now that I was aware of Samantha's deception and Cortiz's schemes. Perhaps it had always been there, simmering, unnoticed; these discoveries peeled back the facade. Dinner was called, and Dr. Archer unexpectedly emerged from his tent. Daniel joined, his cool glance making it clear he was still angry about my stunt with the boat.

We gathered at the long white folding table, its surface scuffed from weeks of use. I took the left aisle seat, facing north, Daniel to my right, Maria beside him, her chestnut eyes avoiding mine. Dr. Archer claimed the seat at the head of the table. Evelyn sat across from me, and Samantha, withdrawn, sat to Evelyn's left, facing south, with Dr. McAdoo beside her. It felt like a silent battlefield, our seats reflecting unspoken alliances.

Bowls of heated canned chili steamed before us, paired with pineapple juice—a welcome shift from the seemingly endless fruit punch. The chili's warmth contrasted with the coldness of the group, set against the din of the jungle as a constant backdrop. Maria's silence was grating. Her expertise with glyphs stood like a wall between us, and her smirk at the temple still stung.

I burned to ask questions, Samantha's lies like a splinter in my mind. I sparked a conversation about Mexico City, its museums, and vibrant streets. The group engaged, their voices overlapping, but Samantha remained silent, her emerald eyes fixed on her bowl. Her isolation was palpable, a crack in her facade.

I turned to her, my voice steady and innocently asked, "You're from Mexico City, aren't you, Samantha?" Her head snapped up in surprise.

"I don't recall telling you that," she hissed, her gold butterfly bracelet glinting as her hand tensed.

"You mentioned it," I said more confidently than I felt. "Which university did you attend there?"

The question hung in the air, sharp and deliberate. Samantha looked nervous, her fingers fidgeting. She glared for a moment and then snapped, "I don't have to answer you." With that, she shoved back her chair and stormed off, her yellow sundress a blur in the dusk.

Dr. McAdoo's face darkened. "How could you do that?" he roared, his aqua-blue eyes blazing.

"I just asked a question," I replied, holding my ground.

"Just a question?" he screamed. "You upset her, and you don't care!" His fury was irrational, but I knew it was tied to the love letter, his naivety a wound.

Daniel stood up beside me. "Don't yell at her!" he bellowed. Dr. McAdoo retreated, his face red, fists clenched, and sweat beading his brow.

"Fine, I'll leave since your wife can't be civil," he said with a sidewise glance, storming after Samantha. Evelyn's sad gaze met mine, her empathy a quiet anchor in the sea of discomfort. Maria just smirked, deepening my unease.

Dr. Archer was on the verge of laughter as he broke the silence. "Who cares what he says?" he said, his green-blue eyes glinting. Daniel and Evelyn chuckled, easing the tension, but Maria shrugged indifferently. Her eyes glimmered with secret amusement, not camaraderie—a warning to tread carefully. Was she friend or foe?

I looked at Dr. Archer carefully. I hadn't noticed the tattoo on his right arm: a green snake with arched white wings, mouth agape, daggers for fangs, red flames curling from its jaws, a sun behind its head. A serpent, perhaps Kukulkan. The imagery was chilling. He caught me staring, but his expression was unreadable.

Exhausted, I felt the need to talk with Daniel, but the camp's thin tents offered no privacy. I announced I'd left my compass and camera at the temple. It was a flimsy excuse, but despite his irritation, Daniel agreed to join me in retrieving it. I grabbed my blue backpack, and we left, the jungle's humidity clinging to my skin, Maria's smirk lingering in my mind.

On the trail, Daniel softened, apologizing for his earlier anger. "I was worried something happened to you," he admitted, his hazel eyes earnest. Alone together, the jungle's chorus enveloped us, offering a rare moment of connection. When we got to the temple, I spilled everything: Samantha's meeting with Cortiz, the office files, the love letter. Daniel was as shocked as I was.

He suggested we take the boat to the river stop, where we could gather more information. I quickly agreed, and we headed to the riverbank, where we found the white motorboat sitting in the moonlight. I checked the motor —it was hot and recently used, a sign that something was going on. Little archaeology happened here. It seemed everyone was pursuing their own agenda. Was it related to the sect?

Daniel started the engine, and we made the short trip to the river stop, the murky water reflecting starlight. At this hour, the town was deserted, its stalls silent. We docked on the right, stepping onto the dirt path to the Singing Quetzal Hotel. Daniel opened the black iron gate, revealing a court-yard with a gurgling fountain, white iron tables, and benches under flow-ering bushes.

The hotel's oak arched door creaked as we entered the lobby, a small, near-circular space with oak floors and a winding oak staircase. A crystal chandelier sparkled, and sheer white curtains framed two big windows.

Two guest room doors flanked the left wall. The air was crisp and clear. The oak front desk stood empty, except for Olivia, the clerk, with her short black hair and caramel complexion warm under the light.

Daniel went to her and asked if Samantha Vasques was staying there. Olivia checked the ledger, shaking her head. On impulse, I wondered about Maria Lopez. Olivia looked down and then nodded. "She's here," she said, and offered to give her a message for me. I was stunned that Maria was there—another layer to her secrecy. Her knowledge of glyphs suddenly seemed suspicious.

Daniel urged us to leave, but the door swung open. "Good afternoon, Señor Cortez," Olivia called out. We turned to find Juan Cortiz, a slender man in a white guayabera, jeans, and loafers. His black hair and chocolate eyes framed a face oozing with arrogance, his caramel complexion smooth. We were rooted in shock. His presence tied the brochure back to reality at camp.

At that moment, Senora Rios's voice called from across the river. She was waving wildly at me. "It's good to see you again, Clara. Is this your husband, Daniel?"

I nodded yes, smiling, but I was filled with tension as Juan turned toward the sound. "Hello, Juan," Senora Rios said. "Have you met the Bennetts?"

He turned, his eyes locking on us. "Hello," he said, "I am Juan Cortiz." His voice was smooth—a predator's calm.

Senora Rios took this as a cue, bidding us farewell and expressing her hope that the building permit issue would be resolved soon. Cortiz paused, confusion flickering across his face, his chocolate eyes narrowing. "Oh, I didn't tell you, they work at the archaeology site," Senora Rios added, her voice bright, unaware of the tension she'd sparked.

Juan's gaze intensified, fixing on us clinically, as if we were specimens. Daniel stiffened, his jaw tight, as Juan stepped closer, his loafers silently moving over the dirt. "Are you aware of the permit?" Juan asked, his tone probing.

I feigned ignorance, shrugging lightly. "Not really," I said, my voice calm despite my pounding heart. The lie satisfied him. His smile returned, but it seemed cold and calculated. He took his leave and turned, boarding his sleek speedboat and speeding away to the west, the river swallowing his wake.

Miguel's voice called from across the river. "Join me at Rosalina's Kitchen for dinner?" he offered, his straw hat bobbing. His cheer was a welcome relief.

Daniel declined politely. "We need to return before sunset," he said.

"Another time then." Miguel waved, smiling, as we climbed into our boat.

The return trip was silent, the river's murky ripples reflecting our unspoken dread. Huntuunich's facade of archaeology crumbled—no, what was real were Cortiz's schemes, Samantha's lies, and Maria's secrets. Daniel broke the quiet, his voice low. "We could say our Belize jobs need us back, that we'll return in a few weeks, but not really. Until then, we make plans for an emergency exit. This place could turn dangerous fast."

He outlined precautions. "We have machetes and pocketknives. Carry a knife always. We'll keep machetes with us outside camp and in our tent at night. We might need to flee to the river after dark. Nobody's focused on the survey—except maybe Dr. Archer and Evelyn. They're the only ones we trust." I nodded, his words sinking in.

Daniel continued, "Tomorrow, we'll excuse ourselves to work alone. We can build rafts from branches and rope and hide them near the river. We should prepare three or four options in case Dr. Archer or Evelyn joins us. If someone else finds them, they might destroy or take them. Keep quiet about what you know. Cortiz thinks we're clueless, but he'll test us. And keep an eye on Dr. McAdoo—he's a lovesick fool, and his blindness makes him dangerous." He said he'd download the office pictures tonight, emailing our family a warning, masking it as routine work.

I felt numb. Daniel's carefree smile was gone, replaced by etched worry, his hazel eyes shadowy and narrow. "We request dismissal tomorrow," I urged. "This won't get better. We need to leave soon."

Daniel nodded, agreeing to email the request and build the rafts. "Tell me everything, even small things," he said thoughtfully. "Our lives depend on it."

I suggested limiting contact with the others, especially with Maria. "Work together, exclude her—out of sight, out of mind," I said. I didn't understand why she'd been in that hotel room, but I remembered her smirk.

"We need to stay off everyone's radar until the helicopter arrives," Daniel agreed. We reached the river's camp exit, finding it deserted. We cut the engine, drifting 15 minutes to the trail, and then pulled the boat back to its original spot. The motor was still warm, hinting at sect activity.

We hurried to our tents. Daniel downloaded the pictures in the office tent, while I slipped the machetes into our sleeping tent, tucking them above our pillows in their sheaths, hidden in my backpack. The promise of the survey had soured; the only thing I craved now was escape. I urged Daniel to keep our cash on us. I was nearly in tears, but my resolve held me firm.

Sleep eluded us, shattered by footsteps near our tent, a sound that had been absent for weeks. The steps paused, deliberately, as if sensing us. Daniel reached for his machete, and I followed suit, our breaths shallow. We braced for an attack, but the steps moved on and faded toward the forest. For an hour, we lay there, our hearts racing and the jungle's silence mocking our fear. The shadow of a serpent glyph filled my mind.

When dawn finally broke, sunlight filtered through the tent. We gripped our machetes, listening carefully for threats. Daniel emailed the dismissal request, relief flickering as he confirmed our family had received his warning. "Play nice until we're out," he whispered.

The team was buzzing at breakfast, but we grabbed granola bars and water and headed out, claiming we needed to retake glyph photos. But our backpacks held no work tools, only rope for rafts. Our true mission lay hidden.

We gathered branches near the river and made the simple rafts, tying them out of sight. It was exhausting work in the jungle heat. Pausing to catch my breath, I studied the temple. Its south-facing staircase was odd. Erosion revealed a sealed eastern doorway and an old staircase, suggesting that the temple had been reoriented—hiding structures to the north? The plastered ceiling in the roof comb hinted at concealed secrets, possibly tied to the Kukulkan sect.

Suddenly, Daniel motioned for me to be quiet. Someone was walking past the temple. I peered around the left side of the temple and caught a quick glimpse of a female form—Maria. She stopped, looking around. We froze. After a moment, she headed away toward the river. As quietly as I could, I started to follow.

"Are you crazy?" Daniel whispered.

"I want to see if she's going to the boat," I said. A few minutes later, the roar of a boat engine broke through the jungle. I turned to Daniel.

"We can't know it's her for sure," he said weakly. "Sure, we know Samantha's a fraud, but Maria is a well-known archaeologist." He seemed to hear the illogic in his own words. A sickening thought entered my mind.

"What if she's the one walking through the camp at night?"

Daniel just looked at the ground and breathed heavily. "Yeah, I think we need to be prepared for anything at this point."

CHAPTER 7

he jungle's midday heat pressed down as we headed toward the temple for lunch, the air thick with humidity. A motorboat's hum broke the silence, its roar closing in. Daniel steps behind me, touches my back, urging me to duck into the thicket. Maria was near, her boat drifting as she cut the engine and glided to the riverbank. She tugged the white vessel ashore, its navy-blue interior gleaming, and slipped a grocery bag into her pink-and-black backpack before vanishing down the trail.

I wondered if she'd made a snack run, like my impulsive trip. Daniel's gaze hardened. "She has a hotel room," he reminded me. "Why hasn't she checked out? That bag could hold anything—a gun, even." His words jolted me, the jungle's buzz fading. Maria's secrecy, her glyph expertise, a wall between us, loomed larger.

"A gun?" I shouted, disbelief rising. "You don't know her!"

Daniel's voice stayed calm. "Neither do you. We just met her." His logic stung; Maria's warmth had seemed genuine, but her hotel stay and now this bag sowed doubt. What had seemed a rivalry was now a quiet threat.

Voices echoed from the temple as a group gathered for lunch. "Avoid them today," I urged Daniel, fearful of Maria and her intentions. He nodded, but another motorboat's drone approached, heading west. It stopped at the bank, and someone got out, footsteps crunching past our hiding spot. My pulse raced. "Who is it?" I whispered.

"How should I know?" Daniel snapped, his hazel eyes scanning the trail.

The footsteps faded, replaced by loud chatter. We crept closer, spotting Miguel, his straw hat bobbing, inviting the team to Rosalina's Kitchen for lunch.

"We should go," I said, sensing a chance to probe further. Daniel hesitated, wary of exposure, but agreed, fearing our absence might draw suspicion.

We joined the group, Dr. Archer's green-blue eyes meeting ours. "What've you been working on?" he asked. Daniel lied smoothly, claiming we'd been mapping the temple surroundings. Surprise flickered across Dr. Archer's face, but he accepted this explanation, his snake tattoo a faint warning under his sleeve. Maria looked at me, sharp and knowing. Her gaze cut through me, her amusement a challenge.

Evelyn approached, her auburn hair catching the sun. Her smile was strained. She sensed the fracture in the group but said nothing, her honey-brown eyes wary. I wanted to shield her from it all, to take her with us if we fled. We could abandon our gear, take our laptop, and essentials. Her kindness deserved protection.

Miguel led us to the river, where his dark green motorboat was waiting. Daniel volunteered us and Evelyn, earning curious stares from Maria and Dr. McAdoo. We boarded. Miguel's boat pulled ahead of the others, the river's ripples oddly soothing. Evelyn's cheer returned, her face brightening as the jungle blurred past—but it was a fleeting peace.

At Rosalina's Kitchen, we docked on the left, waiting for the group to arrive. Teresita seated us, her brown eyes warm, but a knot formed in my stomach when I spotted Juan Cortiz sitting alone at a back booth. His chocolate eyes scanned us, lingering on Samantha. Her return glance sparked Dr. McAdoo's seething glare, his jealousy brewing like a storm. Maria seemed to enjoy the drama, her faint smirk only fueling my unease.

The group settled in, but Juan's presence electrified the air. Samantha smiled when he paid his check and passed her table. Observing her interest, Dr. McAdoo couldn't contain his fury any longer. She excused herself, slipping outside, with Dr. McAdoo trailing quickly behind. Their voices rose, a heated argument spilling into the street, growing louder until Dr. McAdoo's screams pierced the quiet.

"You pushed for Cortiz's permit to help the locals, you said!" he roared. "Now I see it was all to increase your boyfriend's fortune! I'll never approve it. Leave with Juan. I never want to see you again, Samantha," he spat. "You said you loved m—but you lied! You're just a hairdresser, not an archaeologist. I faked it all for you!"

In that moment, I pitied Samantha. Her tears were indeed real, but the fact that all my painstaking detective work had been revealed so casually like this stung somehow. Juan's voice cut through the din, cold and menacing. "If you won't give me the permit, I'll take it by force," he declared, storming off.

Samantha sobbed as Dr. McAdoo's unrelenting tirade continued, the jungle a silent witness to the surreal scene.

Maria's response was completely different. Her amusement grew, her chestnut eyes glinting, a rival savoring the chaos. Dr. Archer buried himself in the menu, desperately ignoring the scene, while Miguel's shock mirrored my own. Evelyn, devastated, rushed outside, arguing with Dr. McAdoo until he retreated. She stayed with Samantha, comforting her, their voices soft against the restaurant's carved door.

Teresita took our orders. Dr. McAdoo returned to the restaurant and sat eating alone at a back booth. His glare was like venom. Lunch passed in silence, Miguel's hope for a pleasant meal crushed, and his job prospects dimming. When we finished, we boarded his motorboat with Evelyn. Dr. McAdoo forced his way aboard, snarling, "I'm not riding with her." His eyes carried an unspoken threat.

The return trip was tense. Dr. McAdoo sat in the front, staring at the forest. Daniel and I sat behind, while Evelyn was in the rear beside Miguel, who steered silently. The river's beauty felt hollow. When we arrived back outside camp, Miguel sped off, relieved to get away. Dr. McAdoo stomped away, with Evelyn trailing slowly.

Daniel and I lingered.

"Juan's threat worries me," I told Daniel.

"Our dismissal request is in," he replied. "I'll check my email."

Back at camp, he returned to our tent, frazzled, collapsing on our sleeping bag. "Six weeks for a helicopter," he said, his frustration evident.

"Why can't we go with the food drop next week?" I asked, exasperated.

"Be thankful the request is in," he snapped. "Till then we wait and lay low." His irritation stung, but he was right—six weeks was our reality.

Tension permeated the camp. Dr. McAdoo and Samantha were estranged, and her presence no longer made sense as a non-archaeologist. Ever the peacemaker, Evelyn let her assist with photos and data, a distraction until she could leave.

Daniel and I aligned ourselves with Dr. Archer, avoiding Dr. McAdoo and his seething silence. I kept the temple's reorientation—its sealed eastern door and hidden northern structures—secret. The survey resumed, but distrust was pulling us all apart.

Memories of home flooded back, a bittersweet but pleasant tide against the sticky, threatening jungle. I missed the laughter, the ease of shared meals, before Huntuunich's secrets had torn us apart. Daniel and I had met as sophomores at Galen University at the Tomato Patch Café near campus. A waitress mixed up our orders. It provided an excuse, and Daniel spotted my cultural anthropology textbook and struck up a conversation. We quickly bonded over shared majors, our lunches stretching into hours. Then it was library study sessions and movies. Six months later, we were dating. Three years later, we married on San Pedro's beach, graduate students madly in love.

I chuckled, recalling our engagement. During a university dig, Daniel slipped a ring into my dirt screen. I found it, slid it on, and said nothing. He asked if I'd found anything interesting. "Not really," I said innocently. He panicked, sifting frantically, until he saw the ring on my finger.

"Why didn't you say anything?" he gasped.

"It's not that interesting," I said with a grin.

He proposed on the spot. "I'll keep digging for better offers," I quipped, but he knew I was joking, and we both knew how we felt about each other. Our laughter echoed in my mind, a joy that now felt so distant.

At the temple, sketching glyphs, I sensed Daniel and Dr. Archer approach. Dr. Archer's green-blue eyes studied the stones, lost in thought.

"What if we're missing a burial?" he mused. "This temple's secrets don't add up."

Without thinking, I blurted out, "The pyramid might have been remodeled." I winced at Daniel's irritated glance. Maria's smirk at lunch flashed through my mind, taunting me.

Dr. Archer's gaze sharpened. "What do you mean?" Daniel tried to deflect, but Dr. Archer closed in, his intensity unnerving. I hesitated, then led them down the staircase, pointing left to eroded stucco revealing a sealed door's outline, chisel marks trailing its edge. The temple's nine thick levels hinted at a religious design, not a tomb, with thirteen layers merged into nine, an altar or stelae likely removed.

Dr. Archer sighed, frowning, his disappointment cryptic. Daniel suggested we check the temple comb, pulling me away. When we were alone, he whispered, "We agreed to keep quiet. You're too naive."

I was stung by his rebuke, but I defended my urge to uncover Huntuunich's history. "Is the comb photography done?" I asked.

He nodded, and I proposed chipping at the patched plaster, suspecting that the religious temple had been remodeled under later kings, erosion exposing the truth.

The comb had an eight-foot ceiling. Daniel lifted me, my trowel scraping the cream stucco. Vibrant colors emerged—yellow, green, blue, red, black—like Calakmul's murals. Red glyphs bordered a mural, their meaning unclear but tantalizing. "We work slowly," I told Daniel, who wavered, saying we should leave the job for excavators. But my gut insisted otherwise. A discovery could halt Cortiz's permit, saving the site.

Daniel conceded a small test area but warned against NIAH backlash. "What about Dr. Archer?" he added. "He's the survey director. If he disapproves, he could ruin us." His worry deepened. "You're impulsive, reckless," he said, voice tight.

"And you're dramatic," I shot back.

I heard footsteps climbing the staircase—Dr. Archer. He froze, eyeing stucco dust on the floor. Daniel's glance urged caution, but I explained, heart racing. Dr. Archer listened calmly, then agreed, recognizing the power of a discovery to block Cortiz's resort. "Get scaffolding from the supply tent," he said. "We'll access the ceiling properly." A faint serpent glyph, half-revealed, hinted at Kukulkan's shadow. Its secrets were tantalizingly close now.

Dusk fell, and we returned to camp. Maria and Dr. McAdoo were nowhere to be seen. Evelyn and Samantha cooked rice and beans, Evelyn's cheer returning, her auburn hair glinting in the firelight. Samantha, buoyed by Evelyn's kindness, smiled, her tears from lunch forgotten. Maria was another matter. There was still a hostility I did not completely understand.

Dr. Archer leaned close. "Don't mention the ceiling to anyone," he whispered. "If it's nothing, I don't want Dr. McAdoo raging." His caution echoed Daniel's. As I ate, Maria's absence gnawed at me. Her boat runs, and glyph mastery hinted at secrets—the sect?

CHAPTER 8

The morning sun warmed the jungle as we carried scaffolding to the temple, where the stones felt cool under our hands. Daniel and I worked carefully, chiseling away the stucco on the temple's comb ceiling, with each scrape revealing a piece of the past. Fine dust floated in the humid air, catching beams of light. Dr. Archer stood nearby, taking photos and noting details on data sheets. After hours, we uncovered a small section with five Mayan glyphs along the back wall. The work would take months, but the thrill of discovery kept us focused, and we never complained.

The glyphs showed this was a religious temple dedicated to Kukulkan, the feathered serpent deity. I was surprised because Kukulkan's influence was weak in this part of the Mayan world, more common in Teotihuacan as Quetzalcoatl. He served as a messenger between kings and gods, yet locals here saw him as the sun deity's cruel pet. Maria was absent today, and despite our rivalry, I missed her skill with glyphs. Her decision to stay at the hotel seemed like a deliberate act of distancing, which only deepened the quiet competition between us.

Kukulkan's stories differed by region. In the Yucatán, he was a winged serpent whose tongue was burned by the proud sun. In the Calakmul area, people disliked him, which made this temple's dedication odd. Dr. Archer's tattoo—a green snake with white wings, sharp fangs, flames from its mouth, and a sun behind it—matched this imagery, with an Aztec touch in the dagger-like fangs. I mentioned it to Daniel, but he dismissed it as a scholar's love for myth and told me not to overthink it.

We spent the week on the ceiling, our backs aching as we finished the border glyphs. The temple, built just before Huntuunich's collapse, puzzled us because it had been remodeled so soon after construction. The mural started to come into view, bright like Calakmul's art. It showed Kukulkan defeating a king who ignored his worship. The winged serpent's image looked like Dr. Archer's tattoo, but I kept that thought to myself, knowing Daniel would brush it off.

The defeated king resembled Night Eagle from other murals, and his death appeared to be connected to this temple; it was likely his tomb. A woman took his place—Xochitl, his peasant wife—and her rise, though rare, was possible in Mayan culture. Something important had happened here. Maria's absence pushed me to dig deeper. I was determined to prove I could match her knowledge of glyphs.

At lunch, we sat at the base of the staircase and ate rice and beans in the heavy heat. No one spoke, and a strange feeling hung over us, as if we were intruding. I suggested covering the murals with stucco, as they didn't match the story on the ceiling. Dr. Archer agreed and asked us to check the back right corner. I remembered Maria's smirk from that tense lunch, and it spurred me to trust my instincts.

After lunch, Daniel and I scraped the corner, and bits of stucco fell to reveal paint underneath. The murals were hidden, too. Uncovering them would take weeks. My back hurt from looking up while chiseling.

"Stop for now. Take the rest of the day off," Dr. Archer said when he saw our tired faces. We agreed and left the temple, surrounded by the steady hum of the jungle.

At camp, we were grateful for the break. We thought about going to Rosalina's Kitchen, but it was getting dark, and the forest was dangerous at night. Maria and Dr. McAdoo joined us, and we listened to music on Maria's CD player. A cool breeze stirred the warm air, reminding me of San Pedro.

I was raised in an apartment above my parents' restaurant, Café Emilce, which was painted mint green with a white iron balcony. The beachfront patio below, named after my grandmother, was always busy.

My mother's laughter filled those memories. She loved to cook in our kitchen, joking with us, and grew red hibiscus flowers on the balcony, which she placed in a vase by the window or tucked into her auburn hair. The breeze brought those days back in a rush. I felt homesick. Maria's presence felt forced, and her secret hotel stay kept us apart, like a rival keeping her distance.

The next morning, we returned to the temple and uncovered most of the right entrance wall. There was a list of Huntuunich's kings, but the faded paint suggested the temple was older than we had originally thought. Drawings on the back entrance wall indicated that Night Eagle's grandfather had built it, ordered by a neighboring city-state to spread Kukulkan's worship, though it never caught on.

The left entrance wall had only the outline of a sealed door, closed with bricks. The current entrance wall depicted Kukulkan standing over Night Eagle's grandfather, who bowed to him, but the new doorway split the mural. These images seemed like propaganda, a power grab dressed as faith. Something had gone wrong under Night Eagle, leading to Huntuunich's fall. *Why wasn't Maria here?* I wondered. I was sure she knew more than she let on.

The murals hinted at a secret group that built the temple to control Huntuunich, not honor Kukulkan. We removed all the stucco from the ceiling and walls, and Dr. Archer bagged it for testing. He was pleased but curious about who these builders were, their identity hidden like a shadow. The jungle sounds filled the silence as we worked.

Things at camp grew calmer. Juan Cortiz's threats had stopped, and Daniel and I thought about canceling our dismissal request. We still had a month to decide. Dr. McAdoo spoke to me briefly, a small step toward mending our working relationship. The jungle's rhythm felt steady, and things were feeling better, but I couldn't shake the thought of Maria's secret boat trips.

Then suddenly it hit me: Huntuunich and Calakmul had collapsed around the same time, yet Kukulkan had no hold over Calakmul, the region's powerhouse. The temple's builders might have used Huntuunich to weaken Calakmul, but it didn't work. Night Eagle's push for independence, ignoring Calakmul, could have doomed them both.

I wondered if Night Eagle knew about this plot. If he had allied with Calakmul, Huntuunich might have survived. Xochitl, his wife, probably understood the danger. Her role in the mural felt important, as if she held the answers. Maria's absence made me want to outdo her, to uncover what she might be hiding.

We were awakened the next day by Dr. Archer's sharp voice, letting us know that we'd overslept. Our muscles ached from weeks of chiseling, and we needed a break.

We stumbled to the kitchen. Dr. Archer took pity, suggesting we take a day off to visit Bosque, the nearby town. Everyone shared our excitement at the thought.

At breakfast, Evelyn made pancakes from a mix. They tasted wonderful, lifting our spirits. I went to our tent to pick out clothes for the trip. It had been so long since I wore something nice. I chose a blue sundress with white polka dots, grabbed a white straw sun hat, and slipped on my gladiator sandals. I packed sunglasses and some cash in my blue backpack, ready for a day free of scraping and toil.

CHAPTER 9

*D*aniel and I followed the river path, the chatter of our group drifting back to us. He wore a green T-shirt and jeans, and his smile broadened when he saw me in my blue sundress. A cool breeze rustled the trail, and leaves crunched underfoot, blending with the steady jungle noise. The air felt alive, promising a rare day of ease.

Evelyn waved as we neared, her smile bright, followed by Maria's terse nod. Dr. Archer and Dr. McAdoo pushed the white motorboat into the river, its navy-blue interior catching the light. Dr. Archer started the engine, and we climbed aboard. Daniel and I took the back row, Evelyn, Samantha, and Maria settled in the middle, and Dr. Archer joined Dr. McAdoo in front. Daniel gripped the motor's handle, steering us smoothly through the narrow river.

Samantha was dressed simply today, trading her usual flair for a white T-shirt, jeans, and gold designer sandals. Her side braid swung to the right, and her gold charm bracelet, adorned with beads and butterflies, glinted on her wrist. Her understated look hinted at a shift, perhaps because her deception had been exposed and she no longer had to pretend.

Maria, by contrast, shone in a grey tube jumper paired with silver thong sandals. A silver opal ring gleamed on her right hand, and a silver abalone butterfly cuff bracelet hugged her wrist. Her French twist elevated her elegance, her poise like a quiet challenge, deepening our unspoken rivalry.

Evelyn surprised us most, wearing an orange short-sleeve button-down blouse with tan khaki pants. Her English braid framed her face, though she kept her work boots, her only shoes. Her effort to dress up clearly reflected her desire to catch Dr. McAdoo's eye, mirroring Samantha's style in a subtle bid for his attention. She glanced at him frequently. Her happiness, though likely unrequited, was strangely touching. For his part, Dr. McAdoo was wearing his usual tan safari vest over a red T-shirt, cargo pants, and boots, oblivious to her efforts.

Dr. Archer looked relaxed in a navy-blue T-shirt, jeans, and flip-flops, his straw Panama hat adding a youthful flair. His style suited him, a contrast to his stern demeanor at the site. The boat hummed along, carrying us past the familiar river stop toward Bosque, the ejido community I was eager to explore.

The journey grew stifling, the sun's heat reflected off the water, with little breeze to offer relief. I was hot and thirsty. As we neared Bosque, the sounds of the forest diminished, animals scarce near the bustling community. The jungle's edge felt tamer, clearly shaped by human presence.

Boat docks lined the right riverbank, most filled with utility motorboats and a few sleek speedboats. Poorer residents relied on boat taxis for travel. Dr. Archer guided our vessel to an open spot and secured it. We disembarked, following a dirt path under a weathered wooden sign that read "Bosque" in bold black letters, marking the trail's start.

The path wound through dense forest for ten minutes before opening to a clearing. Bosque's buildings sprawled in a chaotic Mayan layout, mostly cream-stucco homes resembling temple combs, though plainer. They were rectangular and modest, about 25 by 15 feet, with low ceilings and heavy square wooden doors that nearly reached the roof.

Homes featured a few square windows with thick ledges, originally glassless but now fitted with panes. The ledges held plants and trinkets, lending charm. Thatched roofs topped each house, and no fences separated properties, though small wooden pens corralled goats, chickens, or occasional donkeys and horses used for farming.

The houses were clustered around ten public wells, the town's water source, prioritizing function over Spanish colonial designs with central churches. Bosque was centuries old, descended from Mayans who had survived Huntuunich's collapse and hid from conquistadors in the depths of the forest. Residents spoke a Mayan dialect, with only a few, like Miguel and Senora Rios, fluent in Spanish. I knew some Mayan but relied on Spanish and English.

The Mayans' written language, lost when conquistadors burned codices, had only recently been revived, and archaeologists had decoded many ancient glyphs. Bosque's history was preserved through oral tradition, a lifeline through centuries of isolation. I was fascinated by the town's resilience, its roots entwined with Huntuunich's fall.

In the southwest, shops and a farmers' market thrived. The Sizzling Comal, a restaurant serving Mayan dishes, stood alongside a grocery store, clothing shop, and pharmacy. Locals bought meat, fish, canned goods, and pasta at the store, but the market buzzed loudest, where residents bartered vegetables, eggs, and goat's milk from their gardens and livestock.

Electricity had only arrived 20 years ago as part of Mexico's push to modernize and boost tourism. Roads, power lines, and gas pipelines aimed to draw visitors, but most tourists flocked to Cancun's resorts, wary of Bosque's isolation and lack of attractions. The ejido community valued its Mayan identity, resisting Mexican assimilation to preserve its culture.

The people of Bosque were warm and smiling when we waved, and they were curious about us. They asked about our origins. Maria and I translated for the group, her ease with the locals sharpening my sense of rivalry.

Women wore traditional tapestry skirts and huipils, like Senora Rios, vibrant as ancient Mayan garb. These peasant-style tops, paired with colorful skirts or shawls, reflected modern fashion with woven flat hats adding flair. Men dressed like urban Mexicans in jeans, T-shirts, or cowboy shirts, some sporting boots and hats, blending old and new.

We chose to eat at the Sizzling Comal, settling on its patio at violet-painted picnic tables. Inside, a counter separated the kitchen from a few tables, and a mini fridge held glass-bottled Mexican Coke, sweetened with cane sugar. The menu was small, but the tamales—steamed corn husks filled with chicken, pork, vegetables, and cheese, topped with salsa—were delicious, paired perfectly with the crisp Cokes.

After eating, Daniel and I strolled to the market, where stalls were filled with handmade goods. I bought a tapestry tote bag adorned with two Mayan men in headdresses surrounded by decorative glyphs—not functional but beautiful. No one else spent money, saving their cash for meals and travel home. I wasn't worried. If funds ran low, Daniel and I could tutor locals in Spanish or English, a fallback we'd used before.

We paused at the river stop on our return, the boat's hum fading as Daniel and Dr. Archer sought snacks unavailable in Bosque. Everyone disembarked, eager to browse the market. As I approached the stalls, I heard Senora Rios calling my name. She hurried over, her tapestry skirt vibrant, and asked about our work and Samantha's well-being. I assured her Samantha was fine, but clarified she didn't have a room at the Singing Quetzal Hotel. Senora Rios looked puzzled, saying that Juan Cortiz's girlfriend was staying there. She assumed it was Samantha. I repeated that Samantha didn't have a room there, and she suggested it might be another woman.

Realization dawned. It was Maria, not Samantha, who was Juan Cortiz's girlfriend. She was the one in the hotel room. A plastic sack rustled behind me, and I turned to find Maria standing there, her chestnut eyes cold. "Daniel's asking if you want anything from the store," she said, her voice flat. Senora Rios excused herself, waving goodbye, and Maria's gaze softened into tears.

"I need to tell you something, Clara," Maria said, her voice low. She explained that she'd come here to find her father, who had left when she was eight, and who was possibly raised nearby. Her hotel room served as a contact point for leads on his whereabouts, kept open even after our team arrived. Before I could respond, Samantha and Dr. Archer emerged, and Maria whispered, "Please keep this secret." Daniel joined us, munching on a refrigerated chocolate bar, delighted it hadn't melted in the heat.

Relief washed over me as we headed down the river, my new tapestry purse in hand. Suddenly, a woman appeared by the Singing Quetzal Hotel, her reddish-orange dress and oval crystal necklace catching the light. Her face reminded me of Xochitl from the temple mural, and her arm was marked with Dr. Archer's snake tattoo. Her gaze fixed on me sternly, sending chills through my spine. Dr. Archer signaled to her to retreat, unnoticed by the others, who were chattering over their snacks.

Guilt washed over me as I recalled chiseling away Xochitl's mural, leaving only Daniel's photos as proof. Doubts gnawed—were we overstepping by excavating the temple? Other site areas needed surveying. But my unease wasn't just about the mural—I wondered if anyone would believe me about this woman's appearance. I ached to tell Daniel about it all, about Maria's confession and the mysterious woman, but the boat's noise and company forced me to hold it in for now.

That evening, unable to contain it any longer, I scribbled the day's events on notebook paper and handed it to Daniel. He replied in pencil, unsure what to make of Maria's story or the strange woman's relevance. I erased our words. Something felt wrong, but I couldn't place it. Maria's secrecy fed my distrust.

Morning brought us to the kitchen, where Evelyn and Samantha greeted us warmly, a rare lightness in their smiles. Evelyn shared the good news: Dr. Archer had granted us another day off for rest. I suggested returning to Bosque, but neither Evelyn nor Samantha seemed interested. Daniel agreed to join me for a Mayan breakfast at the Sizzling Comal—coffee, eggs, cheese, plantains, beans, and tortillas.

Alone on the boat, Daniel and I laughed and talked, the river's calm soothing us. Breakfast was as delicious as we remembered. We met Miguel, who looked troubled.

"What's wrong?" Daniel asked.

Miguel frowned, explaining that Cortiz was riling up the residents of Bosque, claiming we intended to hire outsiders instead of locals, fueling their anger. He was trying to drive us from the site with their support.

"They can't believe him, can they?" asked Daniel.

Miguel sighed, noting Cortiz's wealth and influence, his ability to twist the truth to sway people. He warned us to avoid Bosque if trouble arose, directing us east to Catalina instead, the fourth town upriver. "Find Gloria at the corn mill," he said. "Tell her I sent you." His words chilled me, the threat feeling all too real.

Miguel left to ferry a friend, and Daniel checked his watch, urging us to return. As we departed, we saw local men glaring at us, a stark change from yesterday's warmth. Passing the hotel, I scanned for the Xochitl-like woman, but it stood empty.

When we approached the camp, there were two unfamiliar motorboats on the riverbank, prompting Daniel to cut the engine. We drifted and hid the boat in the shrubs near our rafts, concealing it among the branches.

At camp, we were met with angry shouts—Juan Cortiz and Bosque locals accusing us of excluding them from jobs. Evelyn tried to explain that we were only surveying, that NIAH was handling all the hiring, but Cortiz persisted. Dr. Archer demanded they leave, enraging Cortiz, who stormed off with his group after more yelling. Our team stood stunned, uncertainty hanging heavy in the air.

Dr. Archer called an emergency meeting on site security, suggesting precautions if Cortiz continued stirring up trouble. He advised avoiding Bosque for now, optimistic that the issue would fade. Dr. McAdoo remained silent, visibly shaken, while Evelyn and Samantha seemed hopeful but worried. Maria's indifference, her hotel secret, somehow mixed with Cortiz, unnerved me. Time would reveal the truth.

CHAPTER 10

*J*uan Cortiz's intrusion at the camp left everyone tense, unsure of how to respond. We had a few rifles to fend off wildlife, but Cortiz posed the real threat. Evelyn suggested we distract ourselves since we could do little for now, and everyone agreed to stay close to camp for the day. The jungle felt unusually heavy, a feeling of unease that would not go away.

Daniel and I stayed near Evelyn, Maria, and Samantha, while Dr. Archer and Dr. McAdoo patrolled the camp with rifles. They paced through the tent aisles, scanning the perimeter for intruders. Daniel and I had packed our backpacks with essentials—cameras, a laptop, and all our cash—ready for a quick escape if trouble arose. Maria's indifference yesterday lingered in my mind, reinforcing my suspicion of her secret alliance with Cortiz.

Hours passed without incident, and we gathered around the dining table in the kitchen. The tension slowly eased, conversation stirring as normalcy crept back. Then, a tall young man with light tan skin and brown hair, wearing a red T-shirt and dark jeans, burst onto the camp's western edge. He made odd bird calls, comical at first, until his purpose became clear—a distraction.

From the east, fifteen armed men charged toward us, handguns gleaming in the sun. Evelyn screamed, and Daniel shouted to run for the boat. We grabbed our backpacks and sprinted for the trail to the site. Behind us, the attackers toppled folding tables and chairs, their chaos echoing through the kitchen area as we fled.

Glancing back, I saw two men chasing us. The bird-call man, now serious, gripped a handgun on the left, while a short man in a bluish-purple cowboy shirt, jeans, and cowboy boots pursued on the right. They laughed, mocking us with more bird calls, their guns flashing as they gained ground.

I ran faster than I ever had, my heart pounding as if it would burst. Daniel stayed beside me, Dr. Archer leading, with Maria and Samantha close behind. Evelyn and Dr. McAdoo trailed, struggling to keep up. The jungle's dense tangle clawed at us, but fear drove us forward.

Dr. Archer veered toward the temple, aiming to hide behind it. I followed, and the others instinctively did too. We crashed to a stop behind the stones, my chest aching, breath ragged. I was soaked in sweat, born more of terror than effort. I felt faint, the world spinning as I fought to stay upright. Daniel hunched over, hands on knees, gasping and drenched in sweat. Dr. Archer, barely winded, stood calm, his athleticism mocking our exhaustion. Maria and Samantha mirrored my disarray, while Evelyn and Dr. McAdoo, red-faced and trembling, could hardly stand, their legs weak as if unmoored.

Evelyn, struggling to speak, urged us to go. "Leave Dr. McAdoo and me," she gasped. "We'll slow you down. We have a rifle and can hide."

I refused. "We can't abandon you. Those men want to force us to approve Cortiz's permit. They won't leave soon."

Footsteps crunched in the distance, and Maria shouted, "We're over here!" Shock froze us as she drew a handgun from her backpack, aiming at us. Her betrayal, confirmed, cut deep. "Don't speak, Samantha," she snarled.

Instinct took over. Fueled by adrenaline or morning coffee, I swung my backpack with full force, knocking Maria off balance. Caught off guard, she dropped the gun. Dr. Archer kicked it away, standing to her left, but Daniel yelled, "You should've grabbed it!"

I swung my backpack again, tripping Maria as she tried to rise. Samantha rushed forward, kicking her in the stomach. "Run to the boat!" she shouted. We tore through the thicket toward the river path, branches snapping under our frantic steps.

Two new men spotted us and gave chase. I didn't dare look, focusing only on running. The dense jungle clawed at us, slowing us down. My hands shielding my eyes as I crashed through vines. Time blurred, the chase feeling unreal, as if it were happening to someone else. I was consumed by survival, and for moments, I lost track of Daniel, praying he was near.

We neared the river, and Daniel's scream stopped my heart. I glanced back, fearing he'd been shot, but he was still running. "Are you hit?" I yelled.

"No," he shouted, "I forgot we hid the boat upriver!"

Dr. Archer cursed, and Dr. McAdoo snapped, "If they don't kill you, I will!"

Three gunshots rang out, and we zigzagged to dodge them, the men's evil laughter chilling me. I knew more of Cortiz's gang would arrive soon. Daniel veered right, off the path, toward the hidden boat, and we followed. The thicket thinned, making it easier to see, but shots rang out, spurring us on.

We finally reached the spot where we'd concealed the boat. Daniel and I clawed through branches, heedless of scratched hands, until we found it. Dr. Archer and Dr. McAdoo grabbed the rear, helping drag it to the river. My breath burned in my lungs, fear pushing me beyond exhaustion.

Suddenly, Juan Cortiz sprang from the brush and tackled Daniel. They grappled fiercely. Daniel landed a punch, but Cortiz tackled him again, shoving him into the brush. Daniel hit something solid, then seized one of our rafts, swinging it at Cortiz with all his strength. After four blows, the raft splintered, and Cortiz collapsed, motionless for a moment.

"Shoot him! Shoot them all!"

Dr. Archer kicked Cortiz in the chest and stomach, shouting, "Take the boat! I can't hold him long!" We scrambled to push the boat into the river, desperation driving us as the jungle closed in.

Samantha rushed to lift the boat's left rear, where Dr. Archer had stood, and we shoved it into the river. We scrambled aboard as Daniel fired the engine, Dr. Archer leaping in like a scene from an action film. The boat surged forward, Daniel and I in the back row, his hand steady on the motor's handle. Glancing back, I saw Cortiz and his men reach the riverbank, one muttering they hadn't seen a boat earlier.

Daniel steered east instinctively, heading upriver. Dr. McAdoo shouted that he'd chosen the wrong direction, but Daniel yelled back, "We're going to Catalina—it's our backup plan." Dr. Archer, puzzled, asked when Catalina became the plan, and Daniel, irritation sharp in his voice, snapped, "Since ten this morning." Evelyn asked why Cortiz's men weren't pursuing us. "Juan needs some of us alive for his building permit," I replied, "and our rifles give us an edge on the river."

A question struck me, and I turned to Samantha. "Why did Maria warn you not to speak back there? What was she hiding?" Samantha's eyes welled with tears. "She didn't want you to know she's been with Juan Cortiz, working for the permit. She's his girlfriend."

Dr. Archer turned on her, asking how she knew and why she had stayed silent. Sobbing, Samantha explained, "Maria and I grew up together in Mexico City. Her story about her nurse mother and professor father was a lie. Her family is wealthy—her mom owns an art gallery, her dad runs restaurants. My dad was mayor, then a judge; my mom has a boutique. I worked at Maria's mom's gallery, but she framed me for stealing a painting, promising to clear me if I helped her and Juan."

She continued, "I saw the 'stolen' painting in Juan's office, propped against a wall, and a missing artifact Maria was linked to from another site. She's been looting artifacts for years, selling them on the black market. I should've gone to the police, but I feared they'd bribe them. Maria threatened my father's reputation and hinted at worse—maybe even murder. She's always had that edge."

Stung, Dr. McAdoo asked why she didn't seek help. Samantha admitted Maria's last-minute threat before meeting him in Mexico City had kept her silent, afraid of ruin and violence.

The river stretched wide after a sharp bend, growing from twenty-five to one hundred and fifty feet, a straight path to Catalina. After almost an hour, we docked at the first open spot on the left. Dr. McAdoo's questions remained unanswered, and Daniel's patience was fraying.

"We're looking for the corn mill and a woman named Gloria," Daniel shouted, leading us into Catalina. The town, built in a clearing, had wooden homes with thatched roofs, similar to Bosque but more modern—though less sturdy. No church or courtyard defined its center, but several businesses signaled prosperity. Dr. Archer advised leaving the rifles in the boat to avoid trouble.

We followed a stone sidewalk, Daniel striding ahead, determined to find Gloria. A woman in an orange and red huipil, mid-forties with long black hair, pointed us to the corn mill. The large wooden shed had gapped walls, revealing a grinding machine inside, used by locals to mill corn into flour multiple times daily.

Inside, a woman in a light purple dress with blue flowers greeted us. She was short with light beige skin and shoulder-length chestnut hair. She seemed to be in her early thirties, slightly chubby, with light brown eyes and a round face. Daniel asked if she was Gloria, and she nodded. When he said that Miguel sent us, she paused, glancing down, then forced a smile and beckoned us to follow.

She led us to an open-air structure near the river, its roof supported by four beams over a concrete floor. Women were weaving tapestry cloth, crafting items like my Bosque purse for tourists, dressed in colorful huipils and skirts with cinta hair wraps. A tall, slim man with alabaster skin and sapphire eyes stood nearby, his wavy black hair peeking under a green bucket hat. I smelled coconut sunscreen.

Gloria spoke to him for five minutes, then introduced him to us as Michael Hein, a Mennonite in his mid-twenties. He was wearing green cargo shorts, a blue T-shirt, and leather sandals. He offered us a safe place to stay for the night, motioning us to follow. We hesitated, exchanging wary glances, but trailed him to the river, where he had a motorboat waiting.

Daniel mentioned our boat, and Michael, relieved, told us to follow him. Exhaustion and fear weighed on me, the day's chaos surreal. I longed for a hot bath and rest, not this uncertain journey with a stranger. Maria's betrayal—tied to Cortiz, maybe something darker?—loomed, our rivalry now a life-or-death search for answers.

CHAPTER 11

The river stretched wider by another twenty-five feet as we traveled east for twenty minutes, the jungle's hum guiding us to an extraordinary houseboat. Two stories tall, it gleamed with a vibrant violet hull and a light green shingled roof. Arched leaded-glass windows—fourteen on the upper floor, twelve below—adorned its sides, with two bay windows crowning a room above the front porch. White trim framed each window, lending elegance to its grandeur.

Spanning at least a hundred feet long and twenty feet wide, the houseboat was docked on the river's right bank, its west-facing porch a vision of Victorian charm. White hourglass banisters lined the porch, where hanging baskets overflowed with frangipanis, asters, sunflowers, dahlias, and cosmos. The flowers evoked my beloved red roses, their colors vivid against the violet deck. Four wicker couches stood against the railing, inviting rest.

The arched front door, painted light green, beckoned us. This houseboat, extravagant yet peculiar, felt like a dream born of someone's unfulfilled longing for a grand estate, settled instead on this floating marvel. I was intrigued to know its story. We docked our motorboat beside Michael's on the right bank, the scent of baked chicken, black beans, rice, and fried plantains wafting from within, a welcome change from camp's canned fare and a sign of something normal after all the chaos.

Michael asked us to bring the rifles, promising to secure them in a gun cabinet in the utility room behind the kitchen. We stepped onto the violet-painted porch, its deck and ceiling a bold burst of color that made the green door pop. The door, slightly left of center, was the only break in the porch's windowless wall.

Inside, gleaming oak hardwood floors stretched across the entry room, anchored by a cream-and-plum floral Oriental rug. The space felt like a Victorian museum, frozen in time, with Tiffany lamps, stained-glass picture frames, and delicate vases. Two windows on the left wall framed light plum velvet curtains, tied back to reveal the river beyond.

A Victorian plum-colored couch and two armchairs faced the windows, a mahogany coffee table between them holding a vase filled with cosmos. A curved oak staircase rose at the back, its banisters curling right, concealing a square oak door beneath. To the right, French doors opened to a small room with two armchairs, a stand, and a tea cart, its single window draped in pale pink velvet over another floral rug.

Another set of French doors led to the dining room, dominated by a long mahogany table that could seat twelve. A cascading crystal chandelier sparkled above, and a mahogany china cabinet on the left wall displayed blue willow porcelain. Three windows on the right, with cream floral curtains tied back, bathed the cream-painted walls in light. An oak door at the back left connected to the kitchen.

Michael invited us to sit, then vanished into the kitchen. We could hear pots clanging. He returned with a cream serving dish, followed by a woman carrying two more. She set them down and retreated, while Michael fetched cream plates, silverware, and bottled Cokes. He took the seat at the head of the table, facing the French doors, while the woman sat near the kitchen, their formal seating deliberate.

I sat first on the right, Daniel beside me, then Dr. Archer. Dr. McAdoo took the left's first seat, followed by Evelyn and Samantha. I studied the woman, an enigmatic figure, her beauty rivaling Marilyn Monroe or Elizabeth Taylor. Her flawless, near-alabaster skin glowed, her chestnut hair swept into a French twist. A sleeveless pink ball gown and pearl choker accentuated her jade-green eyes, oval face, and sculpted cheekbones. At 5'7", slender, with full lips and long lashes, she radiated poise, her ears unpierced.

Michael said grace, and the woman opened the dishes: rice and beans, chicken with baked onions, and fried plantains. We passed them formally, the meal's warmth easing the day's fear, though an eerie stillness lingered. Michael introduced Osanna, his wife, whose Cuban grandparents had fled to Mexico before communism seized their estate, leaving them with little but memories.

Osanna's grandfather, once prosperous, had built the original houseboat for his wife, a modest echo of their lost grandeur. Michael crafted this replica to replace the decaying original, honoring her legacy.

After dinner, he led us upstairs to rest, darkness cloaking the river. Their bedroom and bathroom lay downstairs, while four bedrooms awaited above. In the upstairs hallway, Michael flipped on a light, illuminating the dim space. A single door faced the porch room, with six doors lining each side. He guided us to the first left, a cozy room with two back-wall windows draped in parted lavender curtains on a gold rod. A double bed with a lavender bedspread and gold fan-shaped headboard stood to the left.

Sparse but elegant, the room held a pine armoire with painted lavender petunias, flanked by matching nightstands. Daniel and I felt like hotel guests, the room's cleanliness surprisingly soothing. Of the four bedrooms, two had twin beds, while two had doubles. We took a double, Dr. Archer a twin room, Dr. McAdoo another double, and Evelyn and Samantha the other twins.

We were exhausted and didn't explore further. The bed's softness cradled us, and we collapsed atop it, still clothed, me on the left. Sleep claimed us instantly, the jungle's hum a distant lullaby. Maria's betrayal haunted my dreams.

Evelyn and Samantha's laughter woke us, echoing in the hallway. I opened our door, finding Evelyn directly outside, startled. "Sorry if we were loud," she said, smiling. Samantha, to her right, announced breakfast was ready, noting that the bathroom beside our room had spare toothbrushes and toothpaste.

The bathroom was dazzling, with a porcelain garden tub and two back-wall windows with sheer white curtains, the wooden shutters pulled aside to let in the light. A sink and toilet stood to the right, the sink nearest the door. Between the windows, a wicker shelf held purple towels, its lower cabinet stocked with toiletries. I thanked them, truly grateful, ready to face the day.

CHAPTER 12

Samantha and I lingered on the porch of the houseboat, the river's breeze stirring the awkward silence. Sensing my unease, she spoke first, her voice soft. "It's good we're finally talking," she said, apologizing for her prior rudeness. "I was blackmailed into this project and jealous of you. Dr. McAdoo praised your archaeology skills and PhD when you joined."

She sighed, her words heavy with regret. "I earned a cosmetology license because I loved doing hair and makeup, but my parents were disappointed, pushing me to be like my surgeon sister or architect brother. They said I should marry rich, dismissing hairdressing as a failure. It hurt, always being compared. I took a job at Maria's mom's prestigious Mexico City art gallery, hoping to impress them, but they didn't seem to care. Maria's scheme dragged me into this mess for nothing."

Evelyn stepped onto the porch, her smile bright, and sat on a wicker bench, glancing between us. "Ready to do it now?" she asked Samantha.

"No time like the present," Samantha replied.

Evelyn held scissors and a folding chair, explaining she'd gotten them from Osanna, who wanted her hair cut too. They descended the porch steps to the riverbank, where Samantha set up the chair. Evelyn sat, handing

Samantha the scissors. "It's been years since my hair had style," she said, smiling.

Samantha was in her element. She crafted a long bob, transforming Evelyn's look. The elegant cut suited her, and Evelyn's genuine delight offered a brief respite from our fears.

She offered to cut my hair before Osanna's turn. I happily agreed, sitting down in the chair. She layered my wavy hair, adding curl without shortening it much. The result was stunning, and I admired her skill, saddened that her parents couldn't see her talent.

Daniel emerged, suggesting a shopping trip to Catalina, reminding us that all our belongings were still at camp with no clear retrieval plan. "We could use shampoo," I said, catching his eye. He grinned at my haircut.

"It highlights your eyes," he said with a smile. I smiled in return, savoring the light, silky feel —a small joy amid the chaos.

Dr. Archer came in, informing us that the motorboat was nearly empty and needed gasoline. Michael agreed to let us use his boat. Samantha chose to stay to cut Osanna's hair, while Evelyn, realizing she lacked deodorant and shampoo, decided to come along.

We boarded for Catalina, Daniel and I in the middle row, Evelyn in front, and Dr. Archer steering. A calm wind stirred grey storm clouds, and Evelyn battled her blowing hair. She'd lost her tan bucket during our escape from camp. I tied my hair into a ponytail, which held it firm against the gusts but did nothing to stop the mosquitoes, which swarmed over us, drawn by the river, biting my hands and neck despite Osanna's bug spray.

In Catalina, we docked and walked past women weaving tapestry goods, waving warmly. We took a grassy shortcut instead of the stone sidewalk, reaching the pharmacy, a yellow wooden building with a metal roof and a sign reading "Pharmacy" over dark blue double doors. No front windows broke its simple facade.

Evelyn and I browsed the shelves, paralyzed by choice. Daniel and Dr. Archer left to buy gasoline for the boat. We hesitated, unsure if we'd go home tomorrow, and decided to wait before buying. The trip, though brief, lifted my spirits—I hated staying cooped up and relished even a short outing like this.

When he returned, Dr. Archer proposed returning to the camp, saying that Michael supported finishing the survey. "Michael suggested hiring local security," he said. "At least we can retrieve our belongings. Tomorrow, a security team will join anyone who wants to check the camp—it's optional." His confidence unsettled me,

Daniel and I exchanged wary glances. Back at the houseboat, we retreated to our room to discuss the situation. "I'm not sure about this," I said. Daniel agreed. Cortiz's armed gang was fresh in our minds. Dr. Archer's vague security details felt off, and his urgency to return seemed suspicious.

Morning found us on the riverbank with Dr. Archer and Dr. McAdoo, rifles in hand. No one else joined. A utility motorboat approached, carrying ten men with rifles, hired by Dr. Archer from Catalina. Their lack of training worried me—mercenaries weren't reassuring. Why they'd risk this baffled me.

Dr. Archer chose a northern riverbank entry, a quarter-mile from camp, and we hid the boats under branches. We hacked through the dense thicket with machetes, grateful for the site's prior clearing. However, the thick jungle slowed us, each step a reminder of our vulnerability.

We found chaos at the camp—tents trampled, belongings scattered. Cortiz's men had ransacked everything, likely looking for information about the building permit data or valuables. I gathered what I could of our clothes and hygiene items into trash bags, leaving ruined notebooks exposed to the elements. Dr. Archer and Dr. McAdoo salvaged their items, and Dr. Archer handed me a bag for Evelyn and Samantha's tents, mainly yielding clothing.

Daniel was relieved we'd taken our laptop and cameras; they held evidence against Cortiz. "He'd know we have a case if he got them," he said, "plus all our site data." I suspected Maria planned to loot our findings, and Daniel's earlier warning about my naivety still stung. Trusting her had been foolish, but our short acquaintance had hidden her true nature.

We arrived where Maria's tent had been, but nothing remained—not even the tent. My favorite blue-embroidered peasant top and Bosque purse were gone, as were items from Samantha's tent. Maria had plundered our belongings, the petty theft a mocking reminder of her betrayal. I felt a strong urge to leave. The camp felt unsafe.

Dr. Archer wanted to inspect the site but agreed to return tomorrow. Security team members carried my bags and helped launch the boats. Dr. Archer's plan to assess the damage at the site seemed risky, but I reluctantly agreed. The temple's secrets—tied to Kukulkan and Xochitl—were too much to resist.

When we got back to the houseboat, Michael was waiting on the porch in jean shorts, a grey T-shirt, and black flip-flops, his fresh clothes a contrast to our three-day-old outfits. He greeted us nervously, and Dr. Archer, carrying his trash bag, announced another site visit for the next day. Michael's concern seemed genuine, which was puzzling given his supposed support.

"I shouldn't have let you go," Michael exclaimed once Dr. Archer was inside.

Shocked, I replied, "I thought you arranged for us to continue."

He shook his head. "I thought it was crazy," he said. "I never agreed with the idea."

Dr. Archer had lied to us. His obsession with the site, perhaps sect-driven, was alarming. Daniel was clearly angry about his dishonesty. I questioned whether it was a good idea to return to the site. Dr. Archer's lie, Cortiz's threat, and the sect's artifacts all screamed of danger. Yet the temple's unanswered questions—its murals, Xochitl's rise, and the mysteries of time—were equally tempting. Daniel wanted to leave, to go back home, but curiosity nagged at me.

CHAPTER 13

Morning light filtered through the houseboat's windows as we prepared to return to the site. Checking our gear, I realized Dr. Archer's plan was impractical—over half our supplies, stolen by Cortiz's gang, were gone. Only Daniel and I had machetes, and Osanna's laundry facilities had cleaned what little clothing we salvaged. The jungle's hum felt ominous, Maria's looting a bitter reminder of her rivalry.

I wore a powder-blue long-sleeve pullover, navy cargo pants, and boots, my hair in a ponytail. Daniel chose a green long-sleeve pullover, tan cargo pants, and boots. Our tan bucket hats, taken at camp, left us exposed, but I had my sunglasses, safely packed before the attack. Without water bottles, we'd have to rely on the kitchen spigot or restroom sinks to fill Osanna's mason jars—a time-consuming chore.

Evelyn and Samantha shared our frustration. Samantha, having lost most of her clothes to Maria, had it worst. I urged her to stay at the houseboat, as she lacked boots or suitable pants. Evelyn was wearing her orange long-sleeve button-down, tan cargo pants, and boots, but she mourned her lost sunglasses, a Secret Santa gift from her last project. Her quiet resolve stood in contrast to the site's chaos, and I admired her strength amid the setbacks.

Dr. McAdoo stuck to his yellow long-sleeve pullover, cargo pants, and boots, while Dr. Archer opted for a red loose-fitting cotton button-down, light tan cargo pants, and black boots. Their determination felt forced, Dr. Archer's insistence on returning unsettling, seemingly driven by more than the survey.

The boat ride was silent, the tension thick. Behind us, nine security guards in grey "Security" T-shirts, navy cargo pants, and black boots rode a camouflage utility motorboat, three per row. Their presence seemed absurd, a hollow shield against Cortiz's threat, and I questioned Dr. Archer's judgment.

We reached the northern riverbank entry, concealing the boats under branches to avoid getting stranded. The security team split, half leading, half trailing, as we crossed the ransacked camp. Evelyn's face fell at the sight— tents collapsed, belongings strewn everywhere. The forest encroached on the camp, with ocellated turkeys and Yucatan brown brocket deer roaming the clearing. Near the site's trail, Evelyn found her bucket hat, her first smile of the day lighting her features.

Daniel and I reached the temple, pausing to strategize. Our notes and paperwork were gone, leaving only our laptop data. I suggested we check the eastern side for a staircase burial, suspecting Night Eagle's tomb might lay there. Daniel agreed, noting it would keep us busy in the eyes of "the dictator"— Dr. Archer and his overreach.

"How much longer must we endure this?" I asked.

Daniel said Dr. McAdoo had secretly contacted the NIAH, arranging an airlift by week's end, a fact they'd kept hidden from Dr. Archer to avoid interference. Relief washed over me, though the eastern staircase tugged at my curiosity, a puzzle linked to Xochitl and the mysterious sect.

We explored the temple's east side. Daniel estimated that a burial would be centered where the staircase once stood, requiring cranes or professional scaffolding we lacked. I scraped stucco at the base with my trowel, searching for resealed mortar, while Daniel leaned against the wall, biding his time until the airlift.

A grinding sound stopped me cold, a moment that shifted everything. My trowel struck gritty, resealed mortar, the sound echoing like a door to the past. Mayan temples were built from quarried limestone and quicklime mortar, layered with pulverized limestone and carved facing stones, and sealed with stucco. This anomaly demanded exploration.

I dug into the mortar, loosening a foot-long facing stone with little effort. Cold, stale limestone dust poured out. Peering inside the opening, I saw an older temple's staircase, faintly lit by sunlight, with the new structure built over it. Such layering was typical. New kings often raised sacred sites to honor deities, but this felt like something more, something deliberate.

Daniel said it was too convenient, suspecting that Dr. Archer knew more than he was letting on. I grabbed my flashlight from my backpack and removed three more facing stones, creating a two-by-two opening for easy access and light. The hollow interior, lacking backfill, suggested that the new temple merely encased the old staircase, offering no structural support, only cover.

I carefully stepped onto the steep staircase, facing the new temple's outer wall. After forty steps, I hit a stone barrier—the floor of a chamber above. This temple was designed to hide a burial chamber within the old staircase, a clever concealment. I searched for mortar lines with my flashlight, the tight space obscuring details.

Finding a seam, I pried at a heavy stone, limestone dust swirling around me. With effort, I dislodged it, setting it on the step below, and Daniel carried it out. The chamber's promise lured me, but Dr. Archer's motives— perhaps sect-driven—filled me with doubt, reminding me of Maria's artifact looting.

Daniel called me. "Time for lunch," he said. It was well past two o'clock. We sat by the temple's staircase, basilisk lizards eyeing our meal jealously. He was frustrated, insisting we shouldn't excavate.

"I wouldn't normally," I explained, "but Dr. Archer's risking our lives for this tomb. He's fixated on a burial, ignoring the site's broader scope. Most temples aren't tombs."

Dr. Archer appeared suddenly on cue. He noticed my dust-covered clothes. "Any updates?" he asked.

Daniel accused him of pressuring us into improper excavation, violating archaeological ethics by digging without need or preparation. Dr. Archer, unfazed, claimed he was following NIAH orders. We were unconvinced, his evident obsession hinting at a hidden agenda.

I showed him the hidden staircase I'd found, regretting it instantly. Had he not appeared, I would have probably resealed the stones; my trust in the project would have been shattered. But Dr. Archer was pleased. Satisfied with our progress, he called an end to the day's work, and we trudged back to the boat. My arms ached from lifting the heavy stones, and Evelyn's strained expression revealed her struggle to focus, the camp's ruin clearly weighing on her.

Back at the houseboat, Michael, Osanna, and Samantha greeted us from the porch, their warmth a welcome relief after the site's tension. Samantha had washed some of our clothes, and neatly folded stacks awaited on the lavender bedspread in our room. The gesture, small but kind, eased the day's strain, though Maria's betrayal cast a shadow that wouldn't go away.

I crossed the hall to thank Samantha. She was folding clothes on one of the twin beds in her and Evelyn's room. The space mirrored ours, with green and pink floral quilts and curtains parted on a gold rod over two back-wall windows. A pine nightstand with painted pink flowers stood between the beds, and a matching armoire adorned the left wall, its floral doors echoing the room's charm.

Samantha smiled at my gratitude, and Evelyn, now relaxed, admitted she knew about the NIAH airlift planned for the end of the week. "I barely worked today," she confessed. "The security team made me nervous, but really, it's too dangerous to stay. We should leave."

Dinner was quiet, tension simmering below the surface. Dr. McAdoo avoided Dr. Archer's gaze, his silence sharp. We savored Osanna's ropa vieja, a flavorful beef and vegetable stew. She was dazzling in a white full-length ball gown, glass stones cascading down its bust, paired with a glass oval choker and T-strap heels, and her hair in a bun. She resembled a bride, her elegance otherworldly. Michael, in a light blue T-shirt, stonewashed jeans, and flip-flops, seemed unbothered by the contrast, their bond transcending mere appearances.

The next day, we returned to the site and resumed work on the tomb. I tackled another floor stone, loosening it slowly before setting it down. Daniel again carried it out, clearing a hole just wide enough for me to enter. Dressed in a yellow long-sleeve button-down, tan cargo pants, and worn boots—scratches evidencing the project's toll—I hoisted myself up, gripping the stone edge and bracing my feet against the walls, my ponytail swinging.

The triangular chamber was ten feet wide, eight feet long, and six feet high. I pulled my flashlight from my pocket and flicked it on, revealing murals of Night Eagle and his family on the walls and ceiling. The limestone tile floor was bare. A carved sarcophagus, its frieze depicting Night Eagle, dominated the center, confirming this as his tomb, hidden within the old staircase.

The murals on the side walls chronicled Night Eagle's life. The one on the left showed him beside Xochitl on temple steps, he in a red-feathered headdress and leopard cape, she in a red huipil and orange skirt with a blue-green sash. Glyphs revealed that he married the daughter of a Kukulkan priest whose grandfather built the temple to spread a fringe sect's beliefs, prioritizing Kukulkan over mainstream Mayan ideology, though it never gained traction.

Night Eagle wed Xochitl for resources and military power to defy Calakmul, but his brothers opposed her, favoring a local queen. Xochitl's focus on the sect alienated Huntuunich, and the murals suggested the sect's heavy-handed push fueled resistance. A chilling detail emerged: Night Eagle was assassinated by an unknown killer, a truth obscured by the temple's propaganda.

Daniel checked on me, telling me it was past three o'clock. He climbed into the cramped, pitch-black chamber, with Dr. Archer following. He studied the murals, taking notes, then fixated on the sarcophagus, its warrior frieze glorifying Night Eagle. I focused on the murals, but the stale, dusty air grew stifling as the three of us crowded the tomb.

Dr. Archer insisted on opening the sarcophagus, ignoring Daniel's protests about the improper methods. Reluctantly, Daniel assisted, revealing a body wrapped in red cloth, adorned with a red-and-black feathered headdress, a spear, an atlatl, and a blue-painted shield with glyphs of victory. A leopard's sash draped his shoulder, but Dr. Archer's swift lift of the shield uncovered a dagger with a crystal handle bearing the image of a winged snake—the same as his tattoo. He stared, transfixed, hiding it briefly before Daniel demanded its return.

"That's enough for the day," said Dr. Archer, seemingly indifferent. He assured Daniel no harm had been done, but he was oddly eager to return to the houseboat.

CHAPTER 14

$\mathcal{M}$orning found me stiff and sore from two days of hauling stones, uncertainty about the day's work gnawing at me. Daniel and I descended to the houseboat's dining room, where the team sat in their usual places, chatting lightly. Evelyn greeted me with a cheerful "Good morning," and Dr. McAdoo, unusually buoyant, asked how we were feeling. The shift in mood felt surreal, like stepping into another world.

Dr. Archer's absence caught my eye, and I asked Evelyn where he was. "He's researching in his room," she said, "and he's suspended the survey until further notice." Relief flooded over me—I wouldn't have to face the dangers of the site again. With the NIAH airlift only two days away, the ordeal seemed poised for a hopeful end, but Maria's betrayal lingered in my thoughts.

Evelyn shared plans for a farewell dinner at Rosalina's Kitchen, joined by a few security team members for safety. "We want to thank Miguel, Michael, and Osanna," she said, "and end this project positively." The idea felt good to me, a chance to honor those who'd sheltered us.

We lingered at the table for hours, sipping coffee and sharing post-airlift plans. Evelyn longed to visit her family in Greenwich, England, after years away. Her nostalgia stirred my own thoughts of home, a contrast to the jungle's chaos. Samantha, headed to Mexico City, was worried about Maria's threat of blackmail, but she seemed resolved to alert authorities.

Dr. McAdoo planned an extended vacation, joking about dull destinations like Mount St. Helens or shark diving in Australia, a far cry from Huntuunich's peril. His humor lightened the mood, but it made me realize I hadn't considered my next step. I'd just assumed I'd return to my government job, but their plans sparked ideas of a vacation with Daniel, somewhere free of Mayan ruins to cleanse this experience.

Packing for the airlift was straightforward, as our belongings were still in trash bags. Juan and Maria had stolen our suitcases, leaving our room a mess of scattered clothes and gear. Suitcase or not, they were washed and ready, and the simplicity felt liberating.

Daniel and I hadn't been this happy since arriving in Mexico, the prospect of home fueling our anticipation. Over coffee, I suggested a vacation, and he agreed, proposing Spain and England. The idea thrilled me, a chance to escape the sect's shadow and Maria's rivalry, which had escalated from professional to life-threatening.

By four o'clock, we prepared for Rosalina's Kitchen, too weary to dress up. My dress clothes were gone anyway, so I wore a lavender long-sleeve button-down, jeans, and boots. Daniel chose a green long-sleeve pullover, jeans, and boots; the long sleeves serve as a shield against the sun and insects. The demands of the jungle even intruded into our casual moments.

Evelyn wore an orange long-sleeve shirt, a long jean skirt, and brown thong-toed sandals, her hair down with a hint of lipstick—Osanna's makeover touch. She glanced at Dr. McAdoo, hoping he'd notice, but he seemed oblivious, his attention drifting to Samantha, strained by our truce. His gaze revealed lingering tension. I brushed it off, focused on leaving. Samantha, last to join us on the porch, wore Osanna's pink sleeveless maxi dress and gold flat sandals, her simplicity striking without jewelry.

Osanna shone as usual in a green-and-purple checkerboard maxi dress with spaghetti straps, her purple sandals adorned with turquoise beads, complementing a three-strand turquoise necklace. Her French twist was impeccable, her elegance a quiet contrast to our weariness. Dr. Archer's absence surprised me. Dr. McAdoo said he was staying to finish NIAH paperwork, which seemed odd given there was only a day left.

At five, we waited for the security team on the porch. Their motorboat arrived, and we boarded ours, Daniel steering from the back where I sat with him. Evelyn and Samantha took the middle, Dr. McAdoo the front. The river sparkled, birds soaring overhead—some unfamiliar, their grace a fleeting gift. The warm, breezy afternoon instilled a soft longing for the forest's magic.

Rosalina's Kitchen welcomed us, and Teresita was our waitress again. She was saddened to hear of our departure, chatting with us as she took drink orders. Miguel arrived, striking in a white cowboy shirt, jeans, a black hat, and boots, with a subtle splash of cologne. His presence grounded the evening, a reminder of the aid he had given against Cortiz and his threat.

We savored our steak tacos, the meal a warm farewell shared with Miguel, Michael, Osanna, and our crew. Laughter and stories flowed, and we avoided mentioning the project's likely end, cherishing the moment. Miguel urged us to return, unaware that this was goodbye, and the joy we were feeling made it hard to correct him.

As darkness fell, we realized we'd lingered too long. Outside, the river was invisible, pitch-black. Miguel offered to guide us to the houseboat, with Michael suggesting he stay if it grew late. The security team, less river-savvy, relied on Miguel's expertise to navigate the unlit waters, where motorboats risked grounding.

The journey was smooth until we neared the site's old river exit. We were suddenly hit with a blinding spotlight from the riverbank, disorienting everyone, including the security team. I shielded my eyes, but Daniel lost control, and the boat ran aground on the right bank. Dr. McAdoo, in front, was hurled into a tree trunk, injured but rising unsteadily. We crashed through thickets, stopped by dense trees and shrubs. Scratches stung my skin in the darkness, unseen but sharp. A man's voice shouted, "They're over here!" Panic welled up in me—ambush! It was Cortiz's gang. A gunshot rang out, and we sprinted toward camp, directionless in the night, desperate to escape.

My heart pounded as I shielded my eyes, stumbling over roots on the river path. I called for Daniel, but silence was the only answer. Frozen, I wondered where he was, fear paralyzing me. "Daniel!" Still nothing, the jungle's rustling animals are my only company.

In the chaos, I'd lost the group, perhaps mistaking another set of footsteps for Daniel's. I veered left, toward the site, running endlessly, completely lost without a compass. A faint light ahead drew me forward, growing brighter as I approached. It was coming from the temple, an odd place for anyone to be. Dread washed over me—could it be Cortiz? I debated fleeing to the river, but curiosity overrode my fear, and I decided to creep closer.

A branch snapped underfoot, and I heard Dr. McAdoo's high-pitched scream, like a horn, echoing nearby. I called out, and he responded from the shrubs, guiding me to the group. Daniel's voice followed, his call a wave of relief. I reached them, and Daniel hugged me fiercely. "Where did you run to?"

"I, I thought I was with you. I was just focused on escaping the gunfire."

We huddled, whispering, as we eyed the light coming from the temple. No one knew who was there, and after what seemed an eternity of waiting, we began to wonder if the threat had passed or if they were toying with us. My curiosity burned, and I moved toward the temple, despite Daniel's protests that it was too dangerous. "We might be stranded if the boat's broken," I argued. Miguel said the security team might have crashed on the left bank, his own boat grounded behind ours.

Samantha joined me, and we led the group toward the light, now flickering like fire. A crashing sound from above froze us in our tracks, fearing another ambush. Evelyn and Samantha screamed as Dr. McAdoo flailed with a stick. He let out a nervous laugh when a squeal revealed a spider monkey rather than a giant snake. We pressed on, shaken but determined.

I climbed the temple steps first, Daniel close behind, urging retreat. The steep ascent was treacherous in the dark, and I tripped more than once, somehow escaping a dangerous fall. As I climbed further, I could hear a male voice chanting inside. When I reached the top, I saw a man sitting cross-legged before a stone altar, fire burning. He wore a green-and-red feathered headdress and held the crystal dagger from the tomb. His clothes were modern—a white cotton shirt, jeans, and black flip-flops—Dr. Archer's clothes. "Dr. Archer?" I called. He looked up, startled.

"How did you find me, Clara?" he asked, eyeing my scratches and the rest of the group. Blood was dripping from a cut on his hand into a ceramic bowl, sticks and matches ready to burn it in a Mayan ritual.

"What are you doing?" Daniel demanded. "Did you use us to get that dagger?"

Dr. Archer added sticks to the fire, his silence damning. "I brought you here, updating the roster to include you, Daniel, Evelyn, and Clara because of your Calakmul expertise. Huntuunich is similar, and I needed you to find the dagger."

"What's so important about the dagger?" Evelyn asked.

History is written by winners, often falsely," Dr. Archer mused. "The conquistador narrative of slaughtering natives is a lie. Some Mayans converted Spaniards to their beliefs without violence, a truth Spain's king buried for glory."

I heard footsteps climbing the steps, and the mystery woman from the hotel suddenly appeared, her blue-and-green zigzag huipil and skirt vivid, crystal necklace glinting. Speaking an ancient Mayan dialect, she argued with Dr. Archer, who responded fluently. I caught fragments—he wanted to relocate the dagger after the Huntuunich discovery, but she forbade it, citing his lack of rank in their society. Dr. Archer scoffed, intent on using the dagger for divine power through a ritual.

Suddenly, Dr. Archer lunged, cutting my forearm with the dagger, drawing blood for the ritual. Daniel lunged to seize it, but the woman tripped him. When Dr. McAdoo tried to help, she knocked him down as well, the altar's dim light obscuring the scuffle.

Looking at my bloodied arm, I shouted, "You were the one sneaking through the camp at night!"

Dr. Archer grinned. "I didn't think anyone would figure that out."

"You were coming here to perform Mayan rituals!"

"Indeed, I was," he leered.

I felt foolish for coming. I lunged for the dagger as he placed it on the fire, but he blocked me. I kicked his leg hard, catching him off guard, and grabbed the handle. The woman turned on me, saying I was forbidden to touch it, and tried to wrest it away. The room spun, her form blurring, and I fell forward, disoriented, colors swirling. Clinging to the dagger, I called for Daniel, feeling a tug on my right hand.

The woman reappeared clearly, her glare piercing as she grabbed for the dagger. Instinctively, I yanked her crystal necklace with my left hand, pulling it off. A blue flash erupted, the dagger vanished from my right hand, and I felt myself falling, collapsing onto a hard stone floor. Pain and disorientation overwhelmed me, and I hesitated to open my eyes, dreading what I'd see.

CHAPTER 15

$\mathcal{M}$y vision blurred as I opened my eyes, the temple's stone floor cold beneath me. I called for Daniel, expecting his voice, but all I heard was silence. Panic rose in me—had I hit my head? A concussion seemed likely; my fall had disoriented me. I shouted for Evelyn, then Samantha, but no one responded. Was I hallucinating? It would be a first for me, and I struggled to grasp what the effects might be.

Gradually, my sight sharpened, the firelight now painfully bright, a tell-tale sign of a concussion. My body ached as sensation returned, as if I'd been struck by a truck. In my hand, the crystal necklace shimmered with a vivid blue hue, humming faintly, its resonance and strangeness unnerving. Dr. Archer's dagger—what had happened?

Footsteps approached, and a man knelt beside me. I called Daniel's name, irritation creeping in at his delay in coming to my aid. But it was a stranger's voice, speaking an unfamiliar Mayan dialect, that asked if I was alright. I saw the man. He had strong Mayan features—long black hair, mocha skin, almond-shaped cocoa eyes. He had an elongated skull, a mark of elite birth, and an aquiline nose framed by full lips. He was of average height and athletic. He studied me with equal curiosity.

I couldn't answer his question about how I'd arrived, my own confusion mirroring his. As I sat up, his kind eyes softened, his voice gentle. His red-feathered headdress was adorned with a conch shell, and he wore a leopard sash over an orange wrap skirt, signaling his importance. Crocodile-tooth necklace, jade ear flares, and a topaz lip plug gleamed, his T-shaped teeth inlaid with alternating jade and obsidian beads.

Dread settled over me as I stood up, wondering if this was a prank, and stepped outside. What I saw chilled me: Huntuunich was pristine, free of overgrowth, its temples and ceremonial center aglow with torches. Stelae and altars lined the plaza, with people bustling through the city-state. Smoke and light rose from the palace and temples, their limestone stucco vibrant and clean, unmarred by the effects of time.

I was in the same temple, but not at the same time. Had Dr. Archer's ritual sent me back? His blood offering seemed incomplete, likely irrelevant, a coincidence. His motives puzzled me—what could he gain? The thrumming necklace suggested that another force had thrust me here, its power bending time.

The stranger introduced himself as Night Eagle, and goosebumps rose on my arms. "Are you Huntuunich's king?" I asked.

His eyes widened in shock. "How did you know? Where are you from?" he demanded.

Hesitantly, I said, "The year AD 2015, by the Mayan calendar."

Disbelief, then fear, crossed his face as he noticed the necklace. "How did you get Xochitl's necklace?" he asked.

"It's a long story," I said, evading the truth.

He offered me shelter, suggesting I pose as a Chontal tribeswoman from the south to avoid suspicion. "Sacniete, a trusted friend, will bring clothes and house you," he said, exiting the roof comb without looking back. Alone, I froze, fearing discovery as an intruder. My thoughts raced to Daniel's fate and then back to Night Eagle's mention of Xochitl's necklace—did he suspect me?

An hour later, I heard footsteps climbing the steps. I stiffened, distrusting Night Eagle's intentions. A woman's voice called out, and Sacniete entered, her blue huipil and green skirt blooming with floral patterns, a matching cinta wrapping her hair. She was slightly chubby, with ruby cheeks and a warm smile. Her round face, aquiline nose, and amber almond eyes radiated kindness. Standing only 5'2", she eyed my modern clothes curiously.

Sacniete handed me a yellow huipil and blue skirt, staring awkwardly before instructing me to change and follow her. She left, and I swapped my clothes, barefoot, as she hadn't provided shoes. Carrying my old outfit, I followed her through Huntuunich's torchlit paths, longing for daylight so I could see its grandeur, a living Mayan city.

She chatted as we walked, asking if I was married. "Yes," I said, and when she inquired about children, I replied, "Not yet." Her warmth eased me, and I asked, "Are you married?"

She smiled, "No, not yet."

Emboldened, I slipped, "Didn't Huntuunich's people want you to marry the king?"

Her shock was brief, but she admitted they had tried. "Xochitl happened," Sacniete said, explaining that Night Eagle found her tall, slim beauty and high status alluring. "I'm a politician with ideas for Huntuunich, but I opposed independence from Calakmul. Xochitl shared his ambition to rival Calakmul and Tikal, so they suited each other."

We reached a cluster of homes, elite limestone structures with stucco and sculptures contrasting with simpler wattle-and-daub dwellings. Sacniete's home, on the right, had a small garden. She called to her mother, introducing me as a royal guest. Ix Kaknab and Aapo, her parents, bore wrinkles and missing teeth from labor but greeted me warmly, both the same height as their daughter and chubby, her mother in an orange-and-blue zigzag huipil and green skirt.

Their home was modest, featuring six hammocks, a hearth for warmth, and a kitchen area for storage, though not for cooking. Woven reed baskets held guavas and tomatoes on a low table, beside ceramic jars and a metate for grinding maize. Reed mats cushioned the floor. Ix Kaknab offered me fruit, apologizing for the simple fare, but I ate from a clay bowl gratefully.

Sacniete's mother spun cotton on a spindle, her backstrap loom nearby, while Aapo farmed and crafted clay vessels for the market. Their contentment shone, despite their hard labor. The empty hammocks, Ix Kaknab explained, belonged to Sacniete's married siblings, now living in nearby homes. Sacniete, in her late twenties, remained unwed, she said, with subtle sorrow lining her voice.

As night deepened, exhaustion washed over me, and Sacniete showed me a hammock, where I slept in the huipil, clutching my old clothes. Thoughts of Daniel twisted in my stomach. I was terrified I'd never see him or home again. Even Maria's presence would be welcome now. I was near Daniel, physically, but separated by time, and my heart ached as I drifted into uneasy sleep.

Morning stirred with Sacniete and Ix Kaknab preparing atole, toasting masa on a comal in the communal kitchen's fire pit. The dough, made from nixtamalized corn, was blended with cinnamon-soaked water, creating a rich beverage. We drank from handleless ceramic cups on a woven mat outside, the drink's chocolate and vanilla notes a comforting start to an uncertain day.

After breakfast, Aapo headed to the fields, taking avocados and beans for a midday snack. Sacniete and I tidied the kitchen, then joined Ix Kakkan in their garden, nestled among the extended family's homes. They cultivated a variety of crops, including tomatoes, pumpkins, chayote, squash, zucchini, gourds, sweet potatoes, beans, and chilies, while also growing cotton for Sacniete's weaving. Her quetzal-patterned sashes and cintas, woven in green and plum, were market favorites.

We washed our hands in a jar by the door, using a woven towel, then gathered inside. Ix Kakkan taught me to use a backstrap loom, guiding my clumsy attempt at a cloth piece. With practice, I might manage patterns, but tomorrow, Sacniete promised to take me to the market to sell her goods, a glimpse into Huntuunich's vibrant trade.

Alone for hours, my thoughts turned to Daniel, my heart heavy with longing. The crystal necklace, hidden in my old clothes, felt like my only hope to return. Fearing it would be recognized as Xochitl's, I buried it under a desert bird bush on the right side of the house, unseen. Sacniete remained unaware, as I'd pocketed it before she arrived.

I practiced weaving, reflecting on my impulsiveness. Daniel once called me naive for expecting honesty, a flaw that events had clearly exposed. Weaving demanded patience—rushing risked ruining the pattern, a lesson in restraint. The loom's rhythm soothed me, grounding my restless mind as I grappled with my displacement.

Ix Kakkan returned to prepare lunch, carrying meat in a ceramic bowl from the family kitchen, along with tomatoes and sweet potatoes. In the open-air kitchen, its thatched roof supported by poles, she sliced tomatoes with a stone blade, hollowing them to stuff with partially cooked meat. She lit a fire under the comal, placed it on three stones, and heated clay balls on a cloth over it, an innovative twist on Mayan cooking.

The heated clay balls, wrapped in cloth, lined a fire pit beside the hearth. Ix Kakkan placed the stuffed tomatoes and sweet potatoes atop them, covering all with banana leaves for slow cooking. The aroma after ten minutes was mouthwatering, a testament to her skill in adapting traditional methods without direct fire contact, unlike typical Mayan practices.

Aapo returned, washing up for lunch. Ix Kakkan served the tomatoes and sweet potatoes on a ceramic plate, with Sacniete adding a bowl of herbs for seasoning, likely shared by her sister who'd pre-seasoned the meat. The extended family's resource-sharing underscored their interdependence, a cultural strength that complemented the meal's delicious simplicity.

After lunch, Aapo worked in the ceramic workshop, crafting a jar using the coil method—rolling clay into strips, stacking them without a potter's wheel. The ancient technique fascinated me, its precision evident in his steady hands. The jars, once shaped, dried to bone-hardness before firing, a process demanding care.

Aapo prepared an open-air kiln, placing jars on a large hearth, surrounded by sticks that he ignited. The fire grew hot and was sustained for hours with added wood. His resourcefulness, born of modest means, impressed me, as he adapted traditional methods to his circumstances, his resilience mirroring Huntuunich's spirit.

I asked why he didn't paint his ceramics. Aapo chuckled, admitting he wasn't skilled at painting, and his children often broke decorated pieces when they were young, so he had stopped. "Some buyers prefer plain wares to paint themselves," he added, revealing a practical understanding of market preferences.

The day's rhythms—gardening, weaving, cooking, and crafting—grounded me in this strange reality, yet the necklace's secret weighed on me heavily. Its connection to Xochitl and the sect hinted at a path home, but Night Eagle's recognition of it made me uneasy. I needed to unravel its power without attracting scrutiny, as my survival at this time was precarious.

Sacniete's hospitality and her family's warmth offered refuge, but my thoughts lingered on Daniel, lost across centuries. The market tomorrow promised an opportunity to learn more about Huntuunich.

CHAPTER 16

I felt excitement stirring as Sacniete prepared to take me to the market, a chance to see the city's commerce in antiquity. She and Ix Kaknab packed a woven basket with sashes and cintas, their quetzal patterns vibrant in green and plum. Aapo added three small clay jars for cooking, their sale a boost for the family's modest income. Sacniete's weekly market trips were unpredictable—some days were profitable, others empty-handed—but today held promise.

Sacniete hoisted the basket onto her shoulder and led me down a sacbe, the "white way" of raised limestone stucco gleaming over rubble fill, a marvel of Mayan engineering. The road buzzed with activity, women balancing baskets on their heads, their fabrics ablaze in red, orange, blue, green, and yellow, a vivid procession under the morning sun.

The market was chaotic, a hollow square of wooden shops with thatched roofs and open fronts, like modern fruit stands. Some boasted colorful canopies, their tables laden with goods, while the central grass hosted plaza vendors on woven rugs. The crowd's clamor was intoxicating. I was experiencing an archaeologist's dream of living history.

Sacniete smiled at a woman approaching us. She introduced her to me as Itzel, a slim woman in her early twenties with long chestnut hair, mocha skin tone, and honey-colored eyes. Her oval face and natural head shape suggested modest origins. She shared her large tapestry rug with Sacniete, a kind gesture given our smaller wares, reflecting Mayan communal bonds.

Itzel sold clothing crafted by her sisters and cousins, supporting their families while they tended to young children. The Mayans' reliance on extended families was evident, and Itzel's role was vital. When I asked if she was married, her gaze dropped, admitting she was, but Sacniete whispered to me that her husband toiled in the king's quarry, overworked by merciless overseers, his health fading.

Noticing Itzel's sadness, I scanned the crowd, noticing many heavy faces. Itzel explained that Huntuunich's three-year drought had spared village greens but ravaged the fields of corn and beans. "Elites take most of our crops, ignoring our struggles," she said, their ritualistic detachment fueling resentment. The people's faith wavered, questioning deities as kings hoarded power. In a hushed tone, she added, "Some doubt our beliefs—what if we stopped rituals? Would anything change?"

Her words revealed a crisis, and I understood why Sacniete was favored as queen. Her empathy contrasted with that of elites, who saw commoners as tools, their semi-divine status blinding them to suffering.

A small boy tugged at Itzel's huipil, and she scooped him up, smiling. Her mother, minding him, checked on her sales, their bond warming the tense market. I wandered alone, marveling at pristine artifacts—clothes, pottery, fruits, and herbs. A jewelry shop caught my eye, its jade and seashell necklaces gleaming, but a crystal necklace, nearly identical to Xochitl's, stopped me cold.

Curious, I asked the shopkeeper, a tall, slender woman in her mid-forties with greying brown hair and a caramel complexion, about its price. She looked at me sharply. "It's not for sale," she snapped. "The queen made it as a gift."

Probing further, I asked about the crystals' source. "Quarried from a local cave," she hissed, "for Kukulkan temple priests and priestesses only, by the deity's command." Her words were a revelation, linking the crystals to the sect and my time-travel, confirming the necklace's forbidden power.

I rejoined Sacniete, relieved I'd hidden Xochitl's necklace, a clear danger in Huntuunich's rigid hierarchy. I heard a commotion. To me, left—Xochitl, wearing a reddish-orange spaghetti-strap dress from my era, hurried into the shop, her crystal necklace glinting. She didn't see me, but her modern attire and haste suggested that the crystals had played a role in my displacement.

Sacniete, having sold all her goods, beamed with pride, successful and ready to head home in triumph. She carried the empty basket on her shoulder, cocoa beans tucked in a pull-string pouch like a purse. The market's energy waned, vendors packing up, and I followed her, the secret of the crystal weighing heavily in my thoughts.

At home, Sacniete stored the basket by the low table in the kitchen, and Ix Kaknab and Aapo celebrated her sales. We worked in the garden until a young man in his late teens, tall and slim with bronze skin and a blue skirt, approached. He was wearing a gleaming obsidian and crocodile necklace. The king had invited me to dine at the palace, and Sacniete's family was welcome to join to host a royal guest.

Sacniete and her parents buzzed with excitement at this rare honor, but dread gripped me. Night Eagle's questions about the necklace and my arrival raced through my mind—could this be a trap? The sect's crystals and Xochitl's presence hinted at scrutiny I couldn't afford; my outsider status was too precarious.

The family bathed and donned their finest clothing. Sacniete shone in a gold-like yellow huipil and skirt with black floral embroidery, her braid woven with golden ribbons. Aapo wore a green loincloth and jade-seashell necklace, while Ix Kaknab chose an orange huipil with red embroidered flowers, a red skirt, and orange cinta, their modesty reflecting their means.

Sacniete offered me an orange and blue zigzag huipil and a blue skirt, the pattern bold yet fitting for the palace. As they prepared, my mind raced, weighing the king's motives against the sect's influence. Dinner promised answers, but at what cost? The crystals' power, tied to Kukulkan's priests, held the key to my return, but Xochitl's shadow threatened exposure.

We passed the market, heading north to the palace, the sacbe's limestone sheen giving way to stucco homes of middle-class artisans. Their flat-topped roofs, sloping like temple combs, stood seven feet high, heavy wooden doors signaling prosperity. The Mayan economy thrived on their craft, a contrast to the drought-stricken commoners' plight, hinting at the Kukulkan sect's divisive influence.

The palace rose on the left, the ceremonial center to the right, its sacbe wider and thicker, a testament to royal grandeur. A multi-level platform, its central staircase—ten feet wide, fifteen feet high—led to the first building, less steep than the temple's steps. The structure's scale dwarfed the surrounding homes, its limestone stucco gleaming under torchlight.

This was Night Eagle's grandfather's home, likely unused, as Mayans buried kin beneath their floors, abandoning houses once all were interred. The two-story, L-shaped building mimicked temple roof combs, featuring a front door that was horizontal to the staircase, a vertical wing with two windows per first-floor wall, and square windows above. Its silent history loomed as we passed.

A rear staircase climbed ten feet, forking left and right around a central wall. Sacniete led us left, ascending another ten feet to a vast home, double the size, with six roof combs. Its complex design featured a single-story entry, a second story behind, and a third on the right, with fewer but larger square windows. The carved wooden door bore Night Eagle's image, glyphs proclaiming the king's residence.

Sacniete knocked, and a servant in a blue-and-yellow floral huipil and skirt opened the door. She was a young woman in her early twenties, and she ushered us to a dining area behind the entrance. The red-painted entry room held a mural of Night Eagle playing a ball game on the left wall, stucco stairs to the second floor on the right, and the space was otherwise bare.

The dining room, painted traditional Mayan blue, was spacious, with windows behind the entrance and on the left wall. Murals of jaguars, monkeys, and parrots adorned the blue walls, vibrant above a multicolored floral tapestry rug. A low central table sat beside a higher one holding jars, cups, plates, and a fruit basket, the room's elegance befitting royalty.

The servant announced Night Eagle and his brother, Sun Jaguar, who entered and sat at the table's head. Unsure of the protocol, we followed: I was on the right beside the king, with Ix Kaknab next to me. Sacniete sat opposite, beside Sun Jaguar, with Aapo to her left. The servant set out fruit, cups, plates, and dishes of guacamole and corn tortillas, the meal's simplicity belying the setting.

Sacniete and Sun Jaguar chatted animatedly, their ease striking. Sun Jaguar, resembling Night Eagle, wore a green-and-blue feathered headdress, leopard sash, red cape, and loincloth. His obsidian necklace and jade-inlaid, T-shaped teeth gleamed, round jade ear flares accenting his bronze skin, long black hair, and cocoa almond eyes, his elongated skull marking elite status.

I spotted the crystal dagger at Night Eagle's waist, tucked between his leopard sash and braided belt. "Where did you get such a lovely dagger?" I asked.

"A wedding gift from my wife," he replied, his tone casual. Before I could probe, he noted Xochitl's absence, citing duties at the temple.

The servant brought tamales and horchata, a rice-milk drink with almonds, cinnamon, and sugar, its light sweetness refreshing. We lingered an hour after dinner, conversation flowing despite my unease about the dagger and Xochitl's sect. Night Eagle finally dismissed us, and we left under a pitch-black sky, the palace staircases torchlit, and the sacbe's white glow guiding us home.

I felt I'd escaped scrutiny too easily, suspecting Night Eagle would summon me again to explain the necklace. For now, the evening was pleasant, the meal and company a respite. The crystals and Xochitl's modern dress haunted me, their time-altering power a puzzle I needed to solve if I ever wanted to return to Daniel.

Back at Sacniete's home, I spent the evening weaving, the backstrap loom's rhythm a balm for my homesickness. Thoughts of Daniel and my family consumed me, the uncertainty of tomorrow looming.

CHAPTER 17

The morning sun spilled golden warmth over the breakfast table as I pushed my plate aside and turned to Sacniete. "I'm heading to the ceremonial center today," I said, my voice steadier than I felt. "It's time I figure out how these crystals work. I need to get home." The temple seemed the logical place to start, its ancient stones whispering secrets I was determined to unravel. Besides, after days of navigating Huntuunich's winding paths, I felt a spark of confidence in exploring alone.

Stepping out of Sacniete's house, I breathed in the crisp air, laced with the scent of blooming ceiba and a faint tang of smoke from distant hearths. The breeze teased my hair as I descended the worn stone steps, sandals slapping softly against the warm rock. Sacniete had pressed a few cocoa beans into my palm—currency for a snack or drink if thirst caught me unawares. The thought of her kindness tugged at my heart, but as the temple's looming silhouette came into view, unease coiled in my stomach. What would I find there? I wished Daniel were here, his steady presence a comfort as we puzzled through this together.

The temple's open doors welcomed the public that morning, a rare reprieve from the elite-only ceremonies that often barred entry. I'd learned the higher one's status, the heavier the ritual burden—especially for the king, whose blood was spilled to appease the gods. The Mayans saw deities in every facet of life, from rain to maize, each demanding constant offerings for the world to turn smoothly. I climbed the steep steps, slower in sandals than my sturdy leather boots, the stone cool beneath my feet despite the sun's blaze.

Inside, shadows cloaked the chamber, the air thick with the scent of copal resin. My eyes adjusted, and the mystery of what had vanished from this temple in my time snapped into focus. A zoomorphic altar of Kukulkan dominated the space, its serpentine form coiled, wings folded over its body, the flattened tips forming a sacrificial platform. Dagger-like fangs gleamed, identical to the blade Xochitl had gifted the king. The realization sent a shiver through me, as if the snake itself was watching.

The roof comb, less ornate than in my era, bore only two murals. On the back wall, one traced twelve generations of Huntuunich's kings, their faces stern in faded pigments. The other, on the side, boasted of the temple's reconstruction by Xochitl's Kukulkan sect, who audaciously claimed to have built it from scratch. The lie was bold, rewriting history in plain sight. I wondered which deity the original temple honored before its influence spread. The altar crouched in the shadowed corner between the murals, unnoticed during my frantic first visit in the dark.

Footsteps echoed up the steps, sharp and deliberate. My heart lurched—Xochitl? But it was the king who entered, his blue skirt swaying, a feathered headdress catching the light like a crest of sapphire flames. His crocodile necklace glinted as he froze, startled to see me. In his hands, a painted ceramic bowl and ritual sticks betrayed his purpose: bloodletting, the lifeblood of Mayan piety, to be burned on the altar. His dark eyes met mine. "Why are you here, Clara?"

I swallowed, the weight of my quest pressing against my ribs. "I came to study the temple. It might hold answers to getting back to my time."

He studied me a moment before speaking, his voice low and measured. "I know you wonder why I'm aiding you. I have questions too, and they may intertwine with yours." He drew the crystal-handled dagger from his waist, its facets catching the dim light. "What do you know of this?"

"It's made from the same crystals as Xochitl's necklaces," I said, my words careful. "They come from a local cave. And I'm certain they're tied to my time travel."

His gaze flickered, a shy, knowing glint that suggested he, too, sensed something amiss with the Kukulkan sect. He exhaled, a heavy sound that carried the weight of years. "I married Xochitl, believing she shared my vision for Huntuunich. Three years ago, just before the drought began, we wed. Some whisper our union cursed this land. Sometimes, I wonder if they're right." His eyes searched mine, raw with vulnerability. "Tell me, Clara, what becomes of Huntuunich? Did I choose wisely?"

The question hung like a blade. If I spoke the truth, would I shatter some cosmic rule of time? I shifted, my sandals scuffing the stone, avoiding his gaze. "This temple..." I began, choosing my words with care. "In the future, it becomes your tomb."

He staggered back, disbelief etching his face. "A tomb? This is a sacred place, not a crypt."

I pressed on, my voice soft but unyielding. "It's remodeled to resemble a funeral temple. The door and staircase shift to face south, not east. The walls are repainted to erase Xochitl and her sect's mark."

He paled with shock. "There's more," I added, hating the words. "You're assassinated. That's how you die."

He sank to the floor, the bowl clattering beside him. Silence stretched, heavy as the stone around us. I knelt, giving him space to process. "Are you all right?" I asked finally.

"No," he murmured, his voice hollow. "I know who will do it. Xochitl and her Kukulkan sect."

A chill snaked up my spine. "Why them?" I asked, though I dreaded the answer.

He lifted his gaze, eyes hard with resolve. "For years, they've pushed to elevate Kukulkan above all deities, claiming their sect holds the true faith. Xochitl resents me for not enforcing their beliefs on Huntuunich. I allowed their temple to stand, but I refused to let her force her will on our people. She's grown distant since."

I frowned, pieces clicking into place. "The dagger she gave you as a wedding gift—why was it so valuable to her sect?"

"It's sacred to them," he said, fingers brushing the blade. "I thought it a gesture of unity. Now I see it was meant to bind me to their cause, to sway Huntuunich over time." His jaw tightened. "We must investigate her and this sect. The crystals are key. We need to understand their power."

"I agree," I said, my pulse quickening. "What's our next step?"

He rose, purpose steadying him. "Tonight, the palace hosts a gathering for the Kukulkan sect. I want you there, Clara. Act curious about their beliefs. They won't probe too deeply on a first visit."

My stomach twisted. "Xochitl might recognize me. In my time, she looked at me like an enemy, though I'd never met her."

He paused, considering. "It's a risk we'll take. To learn about the crystals, you need to visit. Avoid me at the party, and meet me here tomorrow."

I nodded, though dread clung to me like a damp cloth. "I'll go back to Sacniete's and prepare."

"Bring her if she insists," he added, "but fewer eyes on this, the better."

At Sacniete's, I broke the news about the palace invitation. Her face fell when I mentioned it was for me alone. "That's unfair," she huffed, but her hands were already pulling a blue huipil with yellow floral patterns from her chest, pairing it with a yellow skirt traced with blue blooms. "Wear this. You'll fit in."

As I approached the palace, the weight of the evening settled over me. What would I say to explain my presence? Footsteps pounded behind me, and I turned to see Sacniete, breathless, clutching a yellow cinta with blue floral designs. "You forgot this," she said, her eyes tinged with sadness.

"Come with me," I urged, unable to bear her disappointment. Her face lit up, then faltered. "I'm not dressed for the palace," she protested.

"You're perfect," I assured her, and though confusion flickered in her eyes, she fell into step beside me. As we walked, she chattered about the evening, her voice bubbling with excitement, laced with mentions of Sun Jaguar. I hid a smile—she was smitten.

At the palace, guards loomed at the base of the steps. My heart thudded as one fixed me with a stern gaze. "Why are you here?"

"The king invited us to learn about Kukulkan and the priest," I said, praying my voice held steady.

The guard's face softened into a smile. "Pass." A servant in a plain orange loincloth led us up the staircase, past the grand house of the king's grandfather, toward the fork leading to the king's home.

The servant led us to the right, onto a sprawling patio of smooth stucco that gleamed under the fading sun. The open expanse felt precarious, its edges dropping sharply to Night Eagle's grandfather's house below, with no railing to guard the fall. Ahead, a stone wall rose, a narrow staircase curling left to higher structures shrouded in dusk's haze. To the left, two tables stood laden with offerings. One bore ceramic bowls brimming with vibrant fruit and guacamole, flanked by corn tortillas in dishes painted with Kukulkan's sinuous motifs. The other held a clay pitcher of horchata, its sweet cinnamon scent mingling with the evening air, cups stacked neatly to its right.

Torches flickered along the patio's perimeter, their flames poised to defy the coming night. To the right, a small crowd gathered, their murmurs a soft hum against the clink of ceramics. My gaze fixed on Xochitl descending the palace stairs, her blue spaghetti-strap dress—jarringly modern—clinging to her frame. The sight jolted me. Why was she so reckless, flaunting elements from my time? Did she care nothing for the ripples she might cause? Her hair cascaded freely, and her crystal necklace caught the torchlight, its bluish shimmer pulsing like it had when I first arrived. My stomach twisted —she'd used it to slip through time, forward or back.

Xochitl paused, speaking with a young woman whose style echoed her own: long, straight, medium-brown hair, cinnamon skin, and dark chocolate eyes that sparkled with warmth. She was striking, her slim frame and oval face accented by full lips and a straight nose, standing barely over five feet. Xochitl handed her a small gift box, an act alien to Mayan custom, betraying her time spent in my era. The young woman opened it, revealing a crystal necklace identical to Xochitl's. I edged closer, clutching my horchata cup to my cheek, feigning a sip to mask my eavesdropping.

"Visit the council room tonight," Xochitl said, her voice smooth as obsidian. "You're now part of the Kukulkan sect." The young woman beamed, thanking her for the dress, a "coronation" gift for her initiation.

They parted, weaving into the crowd. My eyes drifted to the food tables, where Sacniete stood with Sun Jaguar, their laughter ringing out. Her old huipil, patterned with yellow and green zigzags, bore smudges of garden dirt at the knees, but neither seemed to care. They mimicked each other's gestures, lost in their own world, their joy a bright spark against the evening's weight.

As night deepened, I watched Xochitl lead a group of women up the staircase toward a small structure, its roof crowned with stucco feathers resembling a king's headdress—a private ritual chamber for the royal family. Their voices were hushed. I crept closer, the torchlight casting my shadow long and wavering. Xochitl's voice carried through the door as she welcomed the group, introducing the newest member. Her words turned sharp, dissecting the Kukulkan sect's dual nature. "Some reject Mayan faith entirely," she said, "using it to control the masses, to centralize power. Others believe fervently, recruiting followers to sway society through devotion."

She revealed a chilling truth. "General sect members bear a Kukulkan tattoo on their right arm—like Dr. Archer's." She gestured to her own, a mark she'd taken to deceive the faithful. "They're weak, inferior in their blind belief," she sneered, her voice dripping with disdain. "But true elites are marked by crystal necklaces for women, daggers for men. Only we wield them—never the common members. A true sect member may lack the tattoo but never the crystal."

The conversation shifted to the crystals' power. "Their vibrations distort wavelengths," Xochitl explained. "Long ago, our founders discovered they could disrupt time itself." The new member's voice piped up, curious. "How do we use them?"

"Heat the crystal to go back," Xochitl replied. "Cool it to leap forward. The hotter or colder, the farther you travel."

My pulse raced—I had what I needed. As laughter erupted inside, I slipped away, my footsteps masked by the commotion, the torchlight flickering behind me. I descended the staircase, heart pounding, and found Sacniete still glowing from her time with Sun Jaguar. "Ready to go?" I asked, my voice tighter than I meant.

Her face fell, disappointment clear. "Already?" she said, but she bid Sun Jaguar goodnight, her steps heavy as we left. The weight of Xochitl's words lay heavy on me, a sickening mix of fear and revulsion. Sacniete glanced at me, sensing something amiss, but I couldn't speak—not yet.

That night, the truth burned in my mind. Xochitl had married the king to bend him to her will, to wield religion as a tool for power. But Night Eagle's faith held firm, unshaken by her schemes. She'd realized he'd never yield, that his death or life mattered little as long as her title as queen gave her leverage. I had to warn him—her ambition was a blade poised over Huntuunich's heart.

CHAPTER 18

*T*he morning air buzzed with the hum of Huntuunich as I left Sacniete's after breakfast, my sandals scuffing the stone path to the temple. My heart thudded with nerves at the thought of confronting the king about Xochitl. What if he refused to believe his wife's betrayal? Or worse, what if the truth—time travel, deceit—was too wild for him to accept? I could hide at Sacniete's, wrestle with cooling the crystals alone, and slip back to my time. Yet the king's kindness that first night, when I'd stumbled into this world, bound me to him. I owed him this truth.

Inside the temple, the air was cool, thick with the scent of copal and ancient stone. The king stood waiting, his silhouette stark against the dim light filtering through the roof comb. His face fell when he saw me, a shadow of sorrow in his eyes. "What's wrong?" I asked, catching the frown that tugged at his lips.

"Your return means ill tidings," he murmured, his voice heavy.

I shook my head. "No specific plot against you, but the Kukulkan sect is a lie. The priest and priestess mock the faithful, calling their beliefs foolish. They exploit devotion to spread their influence, ruling in secret, unseen even by kings." I hesitated, then added, "Xochitl's reckless time travel is drawing attention to them."

His brow furrowed, distress etching his features. "My lineage has served Huntuunich well," he said, almost pleading. "How do we stop her?"

I met his gaze, my own unease mirrored in his. "I'm not sure your kings have been as kind as you believe," I said carefully. His eyes narrowed, urging me on. "The people suffer. The drought starves them, yet elites demand full crop tributes, leaving farmers with little. They toil in quarries, felling trees for stucco while the land withers. You should unite resources to ease their burden, not ignore it."

He listened, his jaw tight, each word a blow. I pressed on. "The sect uses crystals to travel time. That's their power." His hand grazed the crystal dagger at his belt, his gaze distant, lost in thought. "What can we do?" I asked.

"I'll consider it," he said, his tone clipped. "I'll tell you later." Dismissed, I left, a gnawing unease settling in my chest. Had I stirred something unstoppable in Huntuunich?

At Sacniete's, the garden burst with color, chilies and tomatoes gleaming under the sun. She waved, her smile warm as I joined her, plucking vegetables for lunch. My mind churned as I grappled with how to cool Xochitl's crystal necklace in the sweltering heat without modern tools. Sacniete's voice cut through my haze, calling my name sharply. A palace guard in a bright orange loincloth stood nearby. "The king will speak at four this afternoon at the Kukulkan temple," he announced.

Sacniete's eyes sparkled, expecting good news. I wasn't so sure but kept silent to avoid suspicion. By three, she insisted we head to the temple, eager for a front-row spot. Such direct addresses from the king were rare, a spectacle for Huntuunich. Ix Kaknab and Aapo stayed behind, wary of the crowd.

The ceremonial center pulsed with anticipation, a sea of bodies pressing close. Sacniete frowned, stuck mid-crowd, scanning for familiar faces. She spotted Itzel and called her over, her son trailing behind. Itzel's excitement matched Sacniete's, though my unease grew. A servant announced the king's arrival, and elites gathered. Sun Jaguar appeared with Snake Smoke, whose Calakmul marriage had strained ties with Night Eagle according to Sacniete. Whispers of a Tikal match for Sun Jaguar were stirring—a bid for Huntuunich's freedom.

Xochitl swept in with fifteen young women, their blue-and-green huipils and matching cintas radiating haughty pride. Xochitl's smile was sharp, performative, oblivious to the king's intent.

The king emerged next, his face somber, silencing the crowd's cheers with a raised hand. He spoke of his lineage's triumphs and Huntuunich's glory, gratitude thick in his voice. Then, his words struck like thunder: He would renounce his kingship to Sun Jaguar. Silence swallowed the crowd. Xochitl's face twisted with shock and rage, her composure fraying.

Some shouted curses, but the king stepped back, unmoved. Sun Jaguar, stunned, stammered that he'd known nothing of this. Xochitl seized the front of the temple, her voice ringing out in an attempt to salvage her sect's hold. Her eyes locked on Sacniete, a venomous grin curling her lips. "The deities declare Night Eagle unfit," she proclaimed, "yielding to Sun Jaguar, who honors Kukulkan. Tonight, we offer sacrifices in worship."

The crowd stirred, uncertain. Xochitl's gaze lingered on Sacniete, marking her as a rival—for what, I couldn't fathom. She strode through the crowd, parting it like a blade, her satisfaction palpable. She stopped before Itzel, glancing back at Sacniete. "The deities demand Itzel's son as the first sacrifice tonight," she declared. Itzel gasped, clutching her son to her hip.

Itzel stumbled back, clutching her son to her hip, her voice trembling with defiance. "Are you mad? He's just a child!"

Xochitl's eyes gleamed, her theatrics swelling. "You question the deities?" she accused, her voice slicing through the crowd. "Itzel defies their will, inviting misfortune on Huntuunich!" She raised her arms, her words a venomous crescendo. "Seize the child! Begin the sacrifice now!"

Sacniete stepped forward, her voice steady despite the tension. "Hold on, Xochitl. You're a priestess of Kukulkan's temple, but you don't command sacrifices. Night Eagle stepped down, naming Sun Jaguar his successor. Only he orders such acts."

The crowd erupted in applause, astonishment rippling through them. Xochitl's gaze narrowed, circling Sacniete like a jaguar stalking prey. "I command the guards to detain the child for Kukulkan's sacrifice," she declared. But Itzel, tears streaming, thrust her son into Sacniete's arms and collapsed before Xochitl, pleading. "Take me instead!" she sobbed, her cries raw and desperate. The scene was brutal, a dagger to the heart; onlookers averted their eyes, unable to bear Xochitl's merciless silence.

Finally, Xochitl spoke, her voice cold. "The child stays. I'll take the mother." Sacniete's face hardened, her words cutting through the air. "You're heartless, Xochitl."

Xochitl froze, her mockery of Itzel's pleas halting. She stepped close, eyes locked on Sacniete's. "If you're so compassionate, why not take the child's place?"

The crowd gasped. Sacniete didn't flinch. "If it stops your unjust, lawless act under the guise of the gods, so be it."

Cheers exploded as the crowd rallied behind Sacniete. Xochitl faltered, surrounded by hostility. She glanced at her Kukulkan followers, but they stood silent, offering no aid. Her face twisted with distress as she retreated to the temple, fixing Night Eagle with a venomous glare. Standing beside him, she addressed the crowd. "Night Eagle has deceived you. He's weak, defying the deities' will. They demand I rule Huntuunich alone, blessed by their favor. Why else has drought plagued us for three years? He must be sacrificed tonight to atone!"

She thrust her arm skyward, expecting cheers, but shock silenced the crowd. "Seize him!" she ordered the guards, who stood motionless, disbelief rooting them in place.

Sacniete surged through the crowd, facing Xochitl eye-to-eye. "Liar! Sorcerer!" she spat. The crowd roared, their respect for Sacniete—humble yet steadfast—outweighing Xochitl's borrowed authority. Was Xochitl's foreign origin her weakness, or simply her arrogance? I couldn't say, but Sacniete held the people's hearts.

Boos rained down on Xochitl. In a flash, she lunged for Night Eagle's crystal dagger, aiming to strike. He caught her wrist, holding her at bay until guards pried the blade free and dragged her toward the palace. All eyes turned to Sun Jaguar, who dismissed the crowd but asked Sacniete to stay. She glanced at me, her nod reassuring me to head back alone.

I lingered, unable to face Sacniete's parents' questions, and wandered the market, its vibrant stalls of woven cloth and carved jade a stark contrast to my loneliness. Thoughts of Daniel and home ached in my chest. An hour later, a commotion drew me back to the temple, where a new crowd gathered. Sun Jaguar and Sacniete stood together, his voice ringing out: as Huntuunich's new king, he would marry Sacniete. They embraced, her joy radiant. I smiled, warmed by her happiness, though surprised by its swiftness.

A guttural hiss cut through the air. Xochitl, torch in hand, stormed through the crowd, her eyes wild. Had Sacniete's rise or her own fall broken her? She climbed the temple steps, turning to the crowd. "Will you deny a devoted priestess her right to worship Kukulkan?" she cried.

A woman's scream pierced the chaos. "Stop her! Xochitl's escaped!" But Xochitl had reached the roof comb, and flames erupted, roaring through the structure. Guards rushed to douse the blaze, but it consumed the temple until it burned out. Night Eagle and Sun Jaguar inspected the cooled ruins— no body remained. Most thought Xochitl burned to ash, but I knew better, as did Night Eagle. This was no accident; perhaps the sect would pin her "death" on Huntuunich. Her influence had waned against Sacniete's.

I approached Night Eagle at the temple's base, his face etched with sorrow. "Are you all right?" I asked.

"No," he said, gazing at the charred ruins. "In your time, was the temple burned?"

I shook my head. "No, it's remodeled after your death, your tomb." His eyes flickered, not with relief but fear. "Xochitl's time travel has altered the timeline," he said, his voice chilling me. "The sect's meddling rewrites history. They must be stopped before they destroy everything for power."

He paused, then confessed, "I found your backpack that first night. Photos of the temple from your time fell out. I searched it, knowing it was wrong, but it showed me Huntuunich's future—rubble. Your restraint in preserving this timeline earned my trust. The sect has no such respect." Regret shadowed his face. "I never asked about your life, your work as a researcher. I see now how vital it is to protect this timeline."

He glanced at the temple. "Sun Jaguar and Sacniete will rule better, easing the people's burdens. I believe Xochitl, in your time's murals, posed as Sacniete to sway Huntuunich after my death—or assassination." He turned toward the palace, and I headed to Sacniete's, bracing for a long night of celebration for her wedding.

CHAPTER 19

*D*awn painted Huntuunich in soft golds as I slipped out of
Sacniete's house, the morning air sharp with the scent of dew
and distant cookfires. My focus on returning home wavered, but I needed
answers about cooling the crystals. Fire sent them backward through time;
now, I had to unravel the cold's secret. With no clear destination, I let my
feet carry me toward the market, hoping the shopkeeper might shed light on
the crystals' mysteries.

The market buzzed with chatter about the royal wedding, stalls over-
flowing with vibrant maize and woven textiles. The shopkeeper stood
outside her wooden shop, her green huipil embroidered with blue jaguars, a
yellow cinta with matching leaf and jaguar patterns adorning her blue skirt.
Her outfit caught my eye, but her snide glance as I approached chilled me.
She retreated inside, her irritation palpable. I softened my approach, wary
of her defensiveness, and browsed the jewelry—jade necklaces strung with
seashells, obsidian beads gleaming beside feathered ornaments. The Mayans
favored such materials over metal, and jade, my favorite, glowed like
captured forest light.

A man entered, his stern presence cutting through the shop's warmth.
His orange loincloth contrasted with a crocodile-and-obsidian necklace, his

bronze skin taut over a muscular frame, geometric tattoos sprawling across his chest. His dark, almond-shaped eyes fixed on the shopkeeper. "No more quarried crystals," he declared. "Night Eagle's orders—no cave activity."

Her face twisted with anger, and a realization struck: She was likely Kukulkan sect, guarding their crystals jealously. Why else resent my curiosity? As the man left, I followed, blending into the market's bustle. He headed toward the ceremonial center, glancing back warily. I trailed him, ducking behind stalls, until he crept along the temple's eastern wall, checking the roof comb and northern corner for watchers.

I darted to the western wall, peering around to stay hidden. There, Xochitl stood, disguised in a modern reddish-brown wig with ringlets, a champagne trench coat, nude heels, and sunglasses, her lips a bold red. The outfit was absurd in antiquity—less a disguise for Huntuunich than for someone from another time. She and the man spoke, his tone pleading, before they moved north, toward an unfamiliar part of the city. I followed at a distance, pausing at fruit stands to avoid suspicion, ready to claim I was offering to Chaahk if questioned.

The stucco buildings gave way to a sacbe stretching into the forest, where howler monkeys screeched and spider monkeys swung nearby, their thuds fraying my nerves. Xochitl's ease in heels betrayed her comfort in modern garb. They reached an eerie cave with twin vaulted entrances, pitch-black and ominous, the sacbe ending abruptly. The sect likely kept this area undeveloped to guard its secrets. Xochitl pulled a flashlight from her coat, its beam swallowed by the proper entrance as her heels echoed on stone. Without light, I turned back, the cave's darkness too daunting.

Near the ceremonial center, I heard Night Eagle's voice calling my name. He stood by the palace, beckoning. "Sun Jaguar and Sacniete are announcing their engagement tonight," he said. "Sacniete's been searching for you."

I shared my sighting of Xochitl and the man at the cave, the sect's crystal source. He urged me to investigate it tomorrow afternoon, when Xochitl would be occupied with rituals, and insisted I not go alone—she was too dangerous.

He led me to the palace's patio, now aglow with torches and fragrant with vanilla orchids in vases painted with Mayan wedding scenes. Tables brimmed with fruit, guacamole, tortillas, and roasted turkey, its savory aroma mingling with horchata's sweetness. Sacniete rushed over, hugging me, eager for my opinion on her wedding dress. Night Eagle handed me my backpack, apologizing for the delay. Sacniete's curiosity flared at its modern design. When he nodded approval, I revealed my time travel, Xochitl's crystal necklace, and the sect's schemes.

Sacniete's eyes widened as I told my tale. Understanding softened her gaze, and Night Eagle nodded. "As future queen, she must know about the Kukulkan sect," he said. Sun Jaguar, too, was privy to their schemes. Night Eagle confessed he'd abandoned his dream of Huntuunich's isolation from Calakmul. "You're right," he told me, his voice heavy. "We need allies. Our seclusion has let the sect grow unchecked."

Sacniete and Sun Jaguar insisted on joining me at the cave tomorrow, arguing that understanding the crystals was vital for Huntuunich's future. My heart warmed at their resolve, yet ached for Daniel and home. The bonds I'd forged here—with Sacniete's laughter, Night Eagle's trust—felt deeper than any I'd ever known. Leaving would break me, yet I wasn't of this time. Why had I been sent to Huntuunich?

The celebration stretched into the night, laughter and torchlight spilling across the palace patio. Sacniete and I returned late with her parents, their joy radiant. Huntuunich would thrive under her and Sun Jaguar, but sadness tugged at me—I'd miss their wedding, their reign. At least Sacniete knew my truth, and I'd bid farewell to her and Night Eagle.

Morning brought renewed focus. I planned our cave expedition, listing torches, digging tools, and weapons in case Xochitl appeared. Sacniete, catching my muttering, assured me the palace had everything. I revealed the crystal necklace buried under her desert bird of paradise bush, her surprise giving way to a smile. Her wedding dress, green with vibrant red and orange floral embroidery, mirrored the bush's blooms. "It's my favorite flower," she said, noting the irony of my hiding spot. "We're bound, you and I."

At the palace, Sacniete's joy shone despite her sadness at my departure. Sun Jaguar and Night Eagle waited by the staircase, and I listed our needs. Sun Jaguar returned with six trusted guards, their presence a shield against Xochitl. We trekked north along the sacbe, my nerves fraying with each step. The forest's cacophony—howler monkeys, snapping branches— heightened my unease. At the cave's twin entrances, Sun Jaguar lit torches, and Night Eagle distributed daggers, his face etched with quiet pain from Xochitl's betrayal.

Two guards scouted the tunnel, calling back that it was clear. Inside, damp limestone chilled my skin, the air stale and heavy. The tunnel sloped sharply, slick under my sandals, nearly sending me tumbling. Torchlight caught a glimmer ahead, revealing a chamber aglow with massive bluish crystals, their quartz-like forms ranging from pencil-thin to pillar-thick. The light danced, bathing the room in ethereal blue.

Mesmerized, we momentarily forgot our purpose until a humming vibration jolted us. Instinctively, I urged, "Douse the torches!" Hesitant, they complied, plunging us into darkness. The hum intensified, and a rippling portal opened, distorting the chamber like water. Xochitl emerged, flashlight in hand, with a man I recognized—a Mexican politician from my time. She explained the crystals' power: a single crystal could teleport in place, but this chamber's multitude allowed travel across hundreds of miles and through time. Cooling crystals in the cave sent one forward; heating them sent one back. "Strike them to vibrate," she told him. "One tap with metal."

I had the key to return home, but feared the attempt. As they vanished through the portal, I rummaged in my backpack, finding my pocketknife. A guard relit a torch, and I tapped a loose crystal, its hum growing as it shimmered blue. Sacniete handed me a torch, her eyes unable to hide her nervousness. The crystal's vibrations shook my hand, pulsing with heat until I released it. It hung suspended, radiating ripples that warped the air. The hum deafened me, drowning out my calls to Sacniete and the others, now lost in the distortion. My dropped torch vanished, and energy pulled me forward, like wind against a sail. I clung to my backpack, eyes shut, and fell, slamming onto rough ground, the crystal clattering beside me.

For ten minutes, I lay still, my heart pounding, terrified to open my eyes. What if I were stranded in a time unknown to me? The crystal's hum faded, and I felt coarse grass beneath me. A soft meow broke the silence, followed by a purr. A white, long-haired cat with green eyes nuzzled my face. I opened my eyes to an oriental rug, pale pink with floral designs, in a colonial-style room. Mahogany furniture, Victorian couches in yellow with rose patterns, and velvet curtains framed French doors to a balcony. A grandfather clock ticked in the hallway, its red rug vibrant against wooden banisters.

Above the fireplace, a wedding portrait stopped my breath. The groom resembled Dr. Archer, beside a dark-haired woman in a white dress. Had I misjudged him? There may have been more to Dr. Archer than I had realized.

CHAPTER 20

I descended the oak staircase, its polished wood cool under my feet, when a familiar hum pierced the hallway below. The sound swelled, vibrating the air with ripples that shimmered like heat waves. A blinding bluish light flared, forcing me to shield my eyes as the house trembled.

"Clara, is that you?" a voice called.

I lowered my hands, blinking. Dr. Archer stood before me, his presence jarring. "What are you doing here?" I asked.

"This is my home," he said, striding toward the kitchen to fetch matches and candles. He lit a white candlestick, its flame dancing in a brass holder, and illuminated the hallway's fixtures, casting a warm glow across the mahogany-paneled walls. "How did you get here?" he asked.

"The crystal in your dagger sent me to ancient Huntuunich," I said, my voice tight. "I don't trust you—you performed that ritual."

He looked at the floor, his tone softening. "It was an act for Xochitl. If she knew the truth, she'd ban me from the Kukulkan sect."

Dr. Archer—Felix Archibeque, he revealed—began his tale. Born in Spain, he joined Cortés's conquistadors in 1518, seeking adventure to prove himself against his father's scorn. But Cortés defied the Spanish crown, attacking indigenous peoples for gold and silver, ignoring orders for peaceful expansion. Greed fractured the conquistadors, and Cortés turned on his own. "He tried to shoot me over my protests," Dr. Archer said. "I fled, saved by a Mayan woman who sheltered me in her village."

There, he immersed himself in their culture, receiving a Kukulkan sect tattoo, unaware of its significance. Cortés tracked him, intent on silencing him. In a fight, Dr. Archer stole Cortés's gold and hid in a cave near Huntuunich, where sect members sent him a century forward. "I used the gold to build this house in Antonella," he said. "I met Isadora, my love, and we married. When she fell ill and died, she hid my crystal here. Losing it could endanger humanity—and my standing in the sect."

His sadness was palpable, but a spark lit his eyes. "Let's find it," he urged. We scoured the house, checking every nook. Inspiration struck—where would someone hide a crystal in plain sight? A chandelier! I ran into the dining room, and there it was, fitted inconspicuously at the bottom.

Dr. Archer explained that Xochitl had sent him to our time to monitor the Huntuunich site, and he had adopted the name Archer and studied archaeology. He was seeking Night Eagle's buried crystal dagger so he could retrieve his own crystal, unknown to Xochitl. "She watched the site, unsettling Evelyn," he said.

He'd found my buried necklace, uncovered by Evelyn, and used it to travel here, suspecting that Xochitl's reckless use of the crystal had shifted the timeline.

"Xochitl's lost the sect's trust," he added. "Her abuse of the crystals draws attention, but as the high priest's daughter, only he can remove her. They're building a case against her."

Changing topics, he told me that Daniel and others had been searching tirelessly for me. "I'd have come if I knew your time," he said, lamenting the crystals' unpredictability.

We needed to return to the cave to cool the crystal. Dr. Archer returned my necklace, keeping his own. We went out to the river and rowed west from his dock, the sun scorching, the oars' rhythm sluggish compared to motorboats.

"Why didn't you save Isadora?" I asked gently.

"Altering timelines risks catastrophe," he said gravely. "Saving one could doom millions." I reflected on my own unintended changes in Huntuunich, guilt stirring.

At the river path, we hid the boat and pushed through dense forest, the ruins of Huntuunich—now cloaked in vines—evoking memories of a burned-out home. Spider monkeys darted through the foliage. Skirting the clearing to avoid ranchers, we neared the cave, its sacbe crumbling under encroaching roots. Dr. Archer lit candlesticks, their flickering light guiding us into the right entrance. We had to move slowly in the dim light.

In the chamber, the crystals' glow was muted. Dr. Archer took his crystal from his pocket and struck it with a metal rod. It started humming, growing louder, vibrating the air, and creating ripples that distorted the darkness with a bluish glow.

A surge of energy swept me forward through time, the cave's outlines blurring as I plummeted, striking the ground with a jarring thud. I kept my eyes squeezed shut, afraid of what lay ahead, but Dr. Archer's movements pulled me from my hesitation. He struck a match against the cave floor, the sharp scent of sulfur flaring as he relit his candlestick, then mine, the warm glow guiding us up the damp incline. His brisk pace left me trailing, my candle's flicker barely illuminating the slick limestone. I wished he'd slow down so our lights could merge. But then the thought of seeing Daniel again sent my heart racing with anticipation—I'd missed him more than words could express. As daylight glowed at the cave's entrance, I glanced at the shadowy left passage, wondering what secrets it held, before stepping into the jungle's embrace.

The sacbe had vanished, reclaimed by tangled vines, and a quiet ache settled in my chest—Huntuunich would forever hold a piece of my heart. We reached the campsite clearing, its scattered tents evoking memories of my last moments here. Though ransacked, it didn't feel abandoned, and hope flickered that Daniel and the others could still be lingering nearby. "What if they've left us?" I called to Dr. Archer.

He glanced back, steady as ever. "We'll follow the river to Michael's houseboat," he assured me, pressing through the forest trail.

A familiar voice—Evelyn's—cut through the undergrowth, tentative yet sharp: "Who's there?"

I broke into a run, weaving past Dr. Archer, my footsteps crunching leaves until I burst into view. Evelyn's scream of fear turned to joy as she recognized me, and I pulled her into a fierce embrace.

"Daniel!" she shouted, her voice echoing. From the temple's roof comb, he appeared, stumbling down the steep steps in his haste, nearly tumbling but catching himself. He reached me, his arms swallowing me, his kiss a lifeline that anchored me home. I'd never felt such joy in his embrace. Samantha emerged from the thicket, her hug warm and welcoming.

"Dr. McAdoo took the airlift," she explained. "The rest of us stayed to search for you." Months had passed, they said. The crystal's timing wasn't perfect, but I was back with Daniel, and that was enough.

I'd once cast Dr. Archer as the villain, assuming he'd abandoned us, but Evelyn set me straight. After my disappearance, Miguel had tackled him, brandishing his rifle wildly, driving off a woman—likely Xochitl. Dr. Archer bared his truth, found my buried crystal in the office, and used it to chase me through time, resolute in his search.

We trekked to the river, where Daniel and Dr. Archer cleared thickets so we could launch the motorboat. I nestled beside Daniel as he steered, Samantha in the middle row, Evelyn, and Dr. Archer in the front. I slipped Xochitl's necklace into my pocket, the weight of safety settling over me in Daniel's presence.

Michael greeted us from the houseboat's porch, calling for Osanna. She descended, resplendent in gold stretch pants, a dusty rose blouse, gold heels, and a pearl choker, her curled hair swaying, and enveloped me in a shocked embrace.

I reveled in Osanna's fried fish, plantains, and carrots, the warmth of Daniel's nearness bringing me home. A knock at the door announced Miguel with fuchsias for Evelyn. Their kiss caught me off guard. "Things changed while you were gone," Daniel murmured with a grin.

We settled around the dining table for coffee, its rich scent a brief comfort. Miguel's visit wasn't just to see Evelyn—he warned us Cortiz had been seen nearby. He suggested stepping away from the site for a while, confident that NIAH's plan to hire from ejido communities would ease tensions in Bosque and undercut Cortiz's influence.

Just then, shouts erupted outside, motorboats buzzing with men hurling curses. Peering through the entrance room's left window, I spotted Cortiz and his gang. Michael and Daniel grabbed rifles, bracing for trouble, while Michael slipped into the cabin to prep the houseboat's engine. He returned, announcing that the anchor was ready to lift, but the dock lines still needed to be untyed. Two gunshots cracked the air. Michael and Miguel stepped onto the porch to face Cortiz, while Daniel stood by the right window, rifle poised. After tense words, Michael moved to untie the boat along the river-bank, Miguel lingering to distract Cortiz's crew. When Cortiz fired at Miguel, Daniel shot back reflexively. We dropped to the floor, all except Daniel; Miguel dove inside, crouching low. Michael, gripping a second rifle, rejoined us as Daniel's shots pierced Cortiz's boats. They took on water and began to sink.

Cortiz steered his faltering boats toward us, aiming to board. Michael fired up the houseboat, its engine groaning as we edged from the dock. Cortiz's stray shots faded in the distance behind us. Michael outlined our escape: We'd head to his town, Marianna, then catch a bus to the airport. Miguel, visibly uneasy, admitted he had no passport, having lived his entire life in the Calakmul Biosphere. "Stay on the houseboat," Michael said warmly, "until I'm back in Catalina."

Michael mentioned a river network on Belize's eastern side, where we'd find a bus to take us home. He'd stay in Marianna, reachable if and when we needed him. The houseboat's engine rumbled, its vibrations pulsing through the floor, as Michael navigated the dark water, floodlights offering faint reassurance. The long, tense night tested our nerves, but Michael's steady hand kept us safe.

We docked at a secluded Belizean vacation spot, free of border checks. Michael paid to moor the houseboat, planning to refuel. Daniel and I decided to lead the group to San Pedro, where my parents' home would offer us shelter. A dock worker pointed us to a bus station two miles away, with a noon departure for San Pedro. It felt like fate aligning. We parted with Michael and Osanna, their friendship a debt we could never repay, and headed to the bus.

Pooling our money, we bought tickets and boarded, sustained by Osanna's hearty breakfast and packed snacks. I caught Daniel's gaze.

"I love you," he said, melting me.

I drew Xochitl's necklace from my pocket, slipping it on, and stared out the window, my thoughts drifting to Juan, Maria, Sacniete, and Night Eagle. Would Xochitl face the sect's judgment? Why did she stare at me that day on the river? What would happen between her and Night Eagle?

The site held answers, but for now, I was excited for San Pedro and my family. As the bus pulled away toward Ambergris Caye, Daniel took my hand—a wonderful feeling I will never forget.